The Children
Paperback Copyright © 2022 Lorhainne Ekelund
Editor: Talia Leduc

ISBN-13: 9781990590238

Give feedback on the book at:
lorhainneeckhart@hotmail.com

Twitter: @LEckhart
Facebook: AuthorLorhainneEckhart

Printed in the U.S.A

THE CHILDREN

Billy Jo McCabe Mystery

LORHAINNE ECKHART

A New Crossover Series!

The Billy Jo McCabe Mystery

Nothing As It Seems
Hiding in Plain Sight
The Cold Case
The Trap
Above the Law
The Stranger at the Door
The Children
The Last Stand

The social worker and the cop, an unlikely couple drawn together on a small, secluded Pacific Northwest island where nothing is as it seems. Protecting the innocent comes at a cost, and what seems to be a sleepy, quiet town is anything but.

The Social Worker

Billy Jo McCabe wants only to help children over-come their troubled lives, as she herself struggles to forget the childhood nightmare she survived. She took sociology and prelaw at the insistence of her adoptive father, Chase McCabe, and learned how to use power tools from her adoptive mother, Rose. She loves reading in the backs of bookstores before tucking the book back on the shelf and slipping out without paying. She has a fondness for peanut butter and dill pickle sandwiches, has a three-legged cat named Harley, hates running (because that was all she did as a kid), and secretly binges on brownies and red wine on the sofa in front of her TV every Friday night.

She's never been married and has dated only twice. She visits Chase and Rose when summoned and shows up dutifully for every holiday with her family, but she has no siblings to speak of, and she feels a growing resentment for the mother who abandoned her in foster care. Despite proudly maintaining the same prickly attitude that nearly landed her behind bars as a kid, she has yet to speak up to Chase, who interferes in her life too frequently, ready to fix every problem, whether she wants him to or not.

One thing no one knows about Billy Jo is that she moved to Roche Harbor because it's the only clue she has about the last known whereabouts of the woman who abandoned her.

The Cop

Mark Friessen, son of Jed and Diana Friessen, has landed accidently in the role of small-town detective, a position in which he's going nowhere. Nearly married once, and broken-hearted three times, he's sworn he'll stay single forever, and he keeps his tattoo of a former girlfriend as a reminder that only fools fall in love. He's tall, attractive, and stubborn, and he refuses to live in the shadow of his two older brothers, Chris and Danny.

As Roche Harbor's youngest detective, he sleeps with a gun under his pillow. He has a stray dog that won't leave, and he swears that the only two food groups that exist are meat and potatoes. His favorite drink is black coffee in the morning, sugared coffee in the afternoon, and a shot of whiskey in his coffee at night to keep him warm.

****Each book in this series is a complete book, with no cliff-hangers, and can be read as a standalone. However, these books may contain references to situations from earlier books in the series. As with any long book series that focuses on specific char-acters, their changing relationships, and how their lives continue to unfold, you may find it more enjoyable to read the series in order of publishing, as there will be developments and changes in the relationship dynamics of the core characters.*

"This is a brilliant thought provoking read that you don't want to be true but we all know it is...A hard hitting story..."

Sally, UK Reviewer

"One thing I have learned about Lorhainne Eckhart's stories is she knows how to take a very relevant and sensitive subject and get the message home...Well written with a very emotive topic."

Caroline L, UK Vine VOice

She picked up the wrong file, and now everything is falling apart.

From *New York Times* & *USA Today* bestselling author Lorhainne Eckhart comes a new Billy Jo McCabe mystery set on a small island in the Pacific Northwest. When social worker Billy Jo McCabe accidentally picks up the wrong file, she discovers a shocking, twisted mystery plotted by a high-ranking social worker in the DCFS.

When Billy Jo McCabe accidentally picks up the wrong file, before she realizes her mistake, she discovers a secret no one was supposed to find.

She takes the file to the newly appointed chief of police, Mark Friessen, but he doesn't believe her—that is, until they discover dozens more files and missing money from vulnerable at-risk children who have aged out of the system and are living on the streets.

As she digs into the files, the system, and the people involved, everything falls apart.

And what Mark and Billy Jo discover is a secret far more shocking than missing money.

———————————

Chapter 1

———————————

"**P**am, I need the Gillespie file. Can you grab it for me?" Billy Jo said as she finished scribbling her notes. When she realized she hadn't heard anything in reply, she looked over to the open door of her office and leaned back in her chair, her laptop open, listening, expecting to hear footsteps, but she heard nothing.

"Pam…" she called out again, scooting her chair way back, looking to the darkened hallway, really listening. But it was quiet.

Too quiet.

She pushed back her chair and stepped into the dimly lit hall to see a darkened front door and no Pam. When she pulled back the sleeve of her navy shirt and looked at her watch, it was only ten after four.

"You couldn't even tell me you were leaving?" she muttered. Pam didn't report to her, but wasn't it a matter of courtesy?

Billy Jo walked over to the file cabinet and pulled open the second drawer, where she knew "G" was halfway down, seeing how packed full it was with paper and files, every one of them signifying a child and family in trouble.

"Gillespie, where are you?" She spotted the thick labeled file and pulled it out, realizing another file had been stuck inside it. She walked the bundle over to Pam's cleared-off desk and opened it to see a stack of papers, with notes written on the inside of the folder, as well.

She pulled out the inside file and spotted "Rae, Deena" scribbled in pen on the tab, and she found herself really looking at all the notes by Link Stone, an older social worker from a year ago or maybe earlier—notes and numbers, with what looked like dollar amounts listed:

$2,384

$1,177

$129

$4,584

She didn't have a clue what any of it meant.

She flicked her gaze to the Gillespie file and then back to the Rae file before unfolding a thick piece of paper from the latter. An envelope slipped out and fell to the industrial gray carpet. She bent down and picked it up.

"What is this?" She took in the folded envelope with "Link Stone" scribbled messily in pencil on the front. It was unsealed, so she opened it and found a check inside, the kind of state check she was familiar with.

The amount of $834 was made out to Deena Rae, and from the color of the check and the date, she knew it was from over a year earlier. "Who is Deena Rae?" she said, recalling the file had been tucked inside the Gillespie file. She flipped the check over again to see that Deena Rae had in turn signed it over to Link Stone.

What the hell?

Billy Jo looked up and over to the tinted industrial windows. This seemed both off and wrong. When her cell phone started ringing, she glanced over her shoulder to her office but turned back to the file, to the check she was holding. She flipped through the pages of notes, looking for an intake form or something, her brow furrowing. There was a photo: dark hair, Hispanic, she thought, and not very old, maybe early teens, with the same haunted mugshot expression she was familiar with.

"Now, why is a check for Deena Rae signed over to you, Link…?"

The locked front door rattled, and then came a pounding. Her cell phone was ringing again, too. She looked over to see her guy on the other side of the door. Mark wore a jean jacket and blue jeans, and damn, did he look good. Check in hand, she strode to the door in her sandals and faded jeans and flicked open the lock.

He pulled the door open, and her heart did a flip-flop. "You didn't answer," he said.

"Sorry, was trying to figure out a mystery." She held up the check and took in his frown in reply. Was this that feeling everyone talked about, that honeymoon phase, where she wanted to spend every second around him?

His gaze lingered, and she wondered if he knew what she was thinking. He reached for the check and really looked at it, turning it over. It was the cop in him that made him too perfect for her. "What is this?"

She started walking, feeling him right behind her, so close. His hand slid over her back as she neared Pam's desk. "I was looking for a file and found this one tucked inside it, for a Deena Rae, whom I've never seen before. That check was in this envelope. Not sure why it was signed over to Link Stone. He was a social worker here a year ago, maybe, I think."

His hand fell away, but he was standing so close to her, looking over her at the file. She didn't need to touch him because there was barely an inch between them, just like when they were sleeping. She never would have believed sleeping next to someone would be something she could get used to.

"I take it this is unusual?" he said. Damn, he was handsome when he was trying to figure something out. This was the man she could see herself with forever.

"Yeah. I mean, what is this check even for? Deena Rae… I'm thinking this is her photo. Young, by the looks of it, and she signed over a check. Why? It hasn't been cashed."

"You know, Billy Jo, it could be for a dozen

reasons. Maybe she didn't have a bank account. You found it in the file?"

She nodded. "Yup, tucked in an envelope right here, with Link's name on it. I don't know, Mark. That doesn't make sense. If a youth is getting a check from the state, she doesn't sign it over to a social worker."

Mark was holding the check back out to her, and she could see he was done with the topic as he glanced to the door and back to her. "You almost finished? I want to grab some dinner. Carmen's on tonight, so thought we'd do a steak and then head home."

And that was it. He wasn't going to ask anything else.

She tucked the check back in the envelope and closed up the file. "Yeah, I'm done. So that's it?"

He seemed distracted. "I'm hungry," he said. "It's a check. You're sure it wasn't cashed?"

Her brow knit. "Yeah," she said. "This is odd."

He let out a sigh. "Look, you said he hasn't worked here in how long? So an uncashed check is stuck in a file. Seems like bureaucracy at its finest. I'm sure there's an explanation, Billy Jo, that doesn't involve us standing here, trying to figure out something that likely happened long ago. Maybe a new check was issued, or maybe it was a mistake. But the last thing I want to do after the day I've had is get tied up in some wild goose chase. Please let's go eat."

She was about to argue with him, and she wondered if that was why he pulled her close, right against him, and then leaned down and kissed her. She entwined her arms around his neck when he pulled back, appearing distracted.

"You okay?" she said. "Something happen today?"

He stepped back, which was also unlike him, and a shadow flickered across his expression. "Just the stress of being chief on an island where it seems like I'm constantly wading into a minefield of politics run rampant. Just once, you know, I'd like to not have to wonder what kind of bullshit is going to come out of the closet." He ran his hand over the back of his neck. He really was not having a good day.

"Council still giving you problems?"

"Seems they're always doing something—but, believe it or not, today it's not them. Seems the state has suddenly flagged Carmen as a homegrown terrorist." He wasn't smiling.

She waited for the teasing, but his pissed-off expression remained in place. "Carmen, our Carmen?"

He angled his head. "My reaction exactly. I spent the rest of the day on the phone, being sent from one career politician to the next as each agency said it wasn't their department. I finally called the Feds, talked with an Agent Kruger in the Seattle office. Seems Carmen Zarko is a common name. I expected him to say he'd fix it, but guess what? It's not that simple."

She knew she was frowning. "And how did you find this out?"

He brushed back his jean jacket as he rested his hands on his hips, those hands that stirred so much in her, and she took in his holstered gun, his badge. "Well, funny thing. I convinced Carmen to take some time off, so she called her sister—you know, the one who has her kid? She worked something out and was going to fly down there, but she went to book her ticket and her name was flagged. She walked into my office, and I've never seen that look on her face before. I told her there had to be an explanation. It seems someone flagged her even though the Carmen Zarko who's supposed to be on the list is a different Carmen, ten years older, and lives in Ecuador, part of some militia. All I got was runaround after runaround, from 'It's not my department,' to 'Sorry, I understand your frustration,' to 'Submit a request in writing to the state department.' But, as the agent I was talking to said, I'll need good luck, because Carmen has a better chance of winning the lottery than getting this fixed." He let out a heavy sigh.

"So…" she started.

"So I told her to take an extra few days and drive. She told me thanks for trying. You know, sometimes, Billy Jo, the incompetence amazes me."

She ran her hand over his arm. "So steak it is," she said. At least now she knew why he wasn't interested in helping her with this mystery.

"And your company," he said as she slid her hands over his shoulders again, feeling how tight he was. He pulled her closer and patted her bottom. "You ready?"

She still needed to figure out why a signed check for Deena Rae was in that file. Then there was the Gillespie file and the paperwork she needed to finish. "Let me just grab my purse and my phone."

He had that brooding look. She knew he was there for everyone. She kissed him again and then stepped away, starting back to the office, before she turned back to him.

"You know, Mark, you can do only what you can do."

He let his gaze linger. "That doesn't make me feel any better," he said. He looked over to the open files she had left on Pam's desk, files she planned to dig into, but tonight she needed to be there for Mark with dinner and a backrub. Tomorrow, she'd figure out what the story was with Deena Rae and the social worker, Link Stone. Opening that file had thrown her into another mystery she knew she wouldn't be able to turn away from.

She grabbed her purse and sweater and tucked her phone inside her bag. When she stepped out of the office, there was her quiet, brooding Mark, holding the check, looking at the file. All she could think of was something her mom had said, that sometimes you had to put aside your own worries to be there for someone you loved.

Chapter 2

Mark hated bureaucracy and red tape. He took a swallow of his coffee, hearing the phone ring in the background. The new dispatcher, Lacy Young, reminded him so much of Gail that he thought they could be sisters. They were the same age, and her confidence in handling the phones and any problems made his job easier. Then there was the new deputy, twenty-two-year-old Elisha Fields, her dark hair pinned back, on the phone, taking a report about what he thought was a stolen bike.

There was a knock on his open door, and he glanced up from the weekly report he was reading to see Carmen in blue jeans and a purple T-shirt, her purse over her shoulder.

"Chief, I'm heading out," she said, wearing the same expression she always did. She really did hide everything she was feeling.

"You take those extra few days and drive safe," he said.

She only nodded, then stepped inside his office. He could see she had something on her mind. "I will, thanks." She closed his door, and Mark leaned back in his chair, hearing the squeak, realizing she was a little on edge. "I wanted to thank you for trying to get me off that no-fly list. You think I have anything to worry about, being labeled a terrorist? I mean, I know how it works, Mark…"

"Hey, it didn't say 'terrorist,' it said 'potential threat'—and it's ridiculous. I'm going to keep working on it. I'll get it squared away. You just go and enjoy yourself. The agent I talked to said it happens more than people realize. Just relax and enjoy the drive. You never know; by the time you get back, it may be sorted out."

She lifted a brow, and he knew she didn't a believe a word he'd said. Neither did he. "That's wishful thinking," she said. "Even I know that someone's clerical error has just basically fucked over my life."

He leaned forward, his forearms on his desk. "Carmen, I promise you it'll get sorted out. The FBI agent I spoke with yesterday, Agent Kruger, is aware now, and he told me to just keep calling everyone, writing everyone, to be noisy and not take no for an answer. People who throw their hands in the air and get frustrated, thinking it can't be fixed, are why this happened to you. I know it's a pain in the ass, but no one is going to come in here looking for you."

He leaned back in his chair as he heard the front

door and spotted Billy Jo. His dog, Lucky, walked over to her, and she made a fuss over him. Carmen glanced over her shoulder to Billy Jo, her expression still doubting.

"Thanks for trying. It's appreciated," she said, then turned to leave just as Billy Jo approached.

"I'm not interrupting…?" Billy Jo said.

Carmen shook her head and gestured to Mark. "Nope. See you, boss," she said. Then she was gone.

Billy Jo took in Carmen and then dragged her gaze back to him, gesturing. "Everything okay?"

He took in her long red coat, which had to be new, black capris, and sleeveless turtleneck underneath. Damn, did she look good. The freckles splashed over her nose and face just made her who she was.

"Yeah, she's just leaving for some much-needed time away," he said.

Billy Jo closed the door, walked around his desk toward him, and leaned against it. His hand went to her thigh, running down over her leg, and she was right there, so close to him.

"So what's up?" he said.

"I know you're really distracted by the Carmen thing. I would be surprised if you got it sorted out."

He didn't say anything, knowing she had something on her mind. "Can't do anything to resolve Carmen's situation right now except keep calling anyone and everyone who could fix it. But I don't have the patience to deal with being continually put on hold or told to call someone else. I get one name and then another until I'm sent right back where I started. So distract me. You can't be done for the day. It's not even…" He lifted his watch to see it was ten after three. "A late coffee break?"

She stared at him, unsmiling. "I can call my dad, fill him in on Carmen's situation. You know he still has the contacts, being who he is, to at least get people off their asses and push you past the roadblocks being set in front of you."

He wanted to say no, but he wasn't a fool. Sometimes it was about knowing that one person who could understand the bureaucracy and fix something. "You wouldn't mind?"

She angled her head and really looked at him before sliding off his desk. "Of course not. It will save you banging your head against the wall and getting nowhere. My dad can make a few calls and then a few more and will accomplish way more in a day than you would in six months."

He knew she was right, and maybe that was what pissed him off more than anything. He lifted his hand, and she stood and strode over to the door. "So that's it?"

Her hand was on the door, and she pulled it open, holding the frame. "Just taking something off your plate instead of adding to it. I'll see you at home?"

Damn, she was perfect. He already felt better. He pushed back his chair, followed her to where she stood in the doorway, and ran his hands over her shoulders and down. "You're perfect, I love you, and thanks."

He leaned down and kissed her, letting his thumbs

brush over her cheeks. She didn't smile, and he could sense something else. He closed the door again and took in the surprise in her expression.

"Okay, tell me what's going on," he said, turning to lean against his desk, crossing his arms, waiting. He knew her so well, when something bothered her or was weighing on her. A case, a kid, anything.

"You have enough on your plate," she said.

He stared at her and pulled in a breath. "Actually, no, I don't. If you recall, you just took the main issue off it. Come on, what is it?"

She made a face, then reached into her purse, pulled out a folded piece of paper, and handed it to him.

"Okay what is this?" he said, unfolding the paper and taking in a list of names. She never played coy. "What is this, Billy Jo?"

She didn't look away. In her blue eyes, which were always so serious, he could see that something really was bothering her. "Remember last night when you came by the office and I showed you that check?"

He stared at her, trying to remember what she was talking about. "That check you found in a file?"

She nodded, then stepped closer to him and tapped the paper he was still holding. "The check was made out to Deena Rae but was signed over to Link Stone. He was the social worker here about a year ago. I asked Pam about it this morning, and she didn't know anything. Deena Rae is a fourteen-year-old girl in the custody of CPS. I made a few calls to the homes she was supposed to be in, and each one said she had been moved. Those names are kids Link Stone was the social worker of record for, and each was getting money from Child Protective Services…"

He shrugged. "Is that unusual?"

She rolled her eyes, something she did when she was frustrated. There was so much about Billy Jo that he knew well, and he realized she never let anything go. "No, payments to kids aren't unusual. It depends on the situation, but they mostly go to older kids who are in special situations. It's something a social worker has to apply for. It mostly goes to the family the child is in care of, for food and clothes. Those names are all kids Link Stone advocated sending money to. Because there are so many, I pulled the files, and I was left wondering why an eight-year-old would need a check, or a three-month-old, who wouldn't even have a bank account. I called up the accounting department to find that they were cashed. Every one of those names had monthly checks issued, including the three-month-old boy, Edgardo Navarro, who died in CPS custody two years ago."

Okay, she had his attention now.

"You sure about this?" he said.

She reached for the paper and took it from him. "Of course I'm sure. I wouldn't be here bugging you about this, knowing everything you have on your plate, if I didn't think there was a problem."

"And it's not some clerical mistake? I mean, CPS isn't exactly known for running an organized agency."

"It could be a mistake, of course. They make them all the time. But that's not the point. The point is that there are too many names, and although I haven't dug into all of them, with the ones I have, I'm seeing something I don't like."

Damn. Kids and animals were the issues he couldn't turn his back on. "What do you want me to do?"

She pulled in her lower lip and bit it, then flicked her shoulder-length hair behind her ears. "There has to be a paper trail. After putting in a call to Grant, I found out Link Stone took a new job in Cody, Wyoming, but when I called the CPS in Cody, they didn't have anyone by that name working there. Can you go into your database and find out where he is? Just a hunch I have, but if I'm right, I hope there's some explanation for this."

He already knew where this was going, and he hoped she was wrong too. "You think he took money from a bunch of vulnerable kids?"

She pulled her arms over her chest, the paper still in her hand. She was so close to him as she shrugged. "I hope I'm wrong, Mark, but that feeling I have in the pit of my stomach that he did it…well, it's there, and it makes me sick."

He stood up and slid his hand over her arm, moving her back as he walked around his desk and pulled open the top drawer to reach for his keys and then his jean jacket on the back of his chair.

"What are you doing?" she asked as he shrugged it on.

"We're going back to your office, where you're going to pull all these files and we're going to go through them. Billy Jo, I swear, I hope you're wrong."

She tucked the paper back in her purse and flicked those blue eyes up to him. "So do I, but I already know I'm not," she said. Then she pulled open the door, and he followed her out of his office.

"Lucky, come on," he called to his dog, who was eating kibble. He looked over to his new deputy, who watched him with wary dark eyes. "Elisha, I want you to do a search on a Link Stone. He used to be a social worker on the island a year ago. Find out where he is now, what he owns, and where he banks, and then call me with everything."

She was scribbling. Billy Jo was watching him, holding the door open.

"Lacy's got my cell phone," he continued. "Call me if anything comes up."

"Will do, Chief," was all Elisha said.

He followed Billy Jo out the door, his dog looking between them, and said, "I'll follow you to your office. You know if you're right, this is really bad."

She pulled open her driver's door, then glanced away, as if thinking, and back to him. "I know, and if it's true, the thing is that CPS will never want the truth to get out."

Damn! Why couldn't this island be a sleepy, quiet place where nothing ever happened? But he already knew the answer. Sleepy, quiet places were the perfect places to keep anything and everything under the radar.

Chapter 3

"You want another piece of pizza?" Billy Jo asked, sitting cross legged in the middle of the office, while Mark was in Pam's chair. The file cabinet was open, and what seemed like every file had been pulled out.

He didn't look over to her as he shook his head and said, "Nope, all yours."

She reached for another slice from the open box beside her. It was dark outside, and the clock on the wall read nearly midnight. She had so many notes, pages and pages.

When she heard the click of the front door, she damn near jumped out of her skin. Mark was on his feet, and Billy Jo turned to see Pam walking in, her hair pulled back in a ponytail, wearing yoga pants.

"Why are you both here?" Pam said. "I was just driving by on my way home, out for dinner with friends, and saw the office lit up. I didn't think I'd left the lights on… Why do you have all these files out?"

She could see Pam was ready to make an issue of this. What was Billy Jo going to say to get her out of there?

"Just researching some things," she said.

Mark, who was still standing behind the desk, lifted a brow to her and then dragged his gaze back to Pam. "Actually, Pam, we're looking into a discrepancy that could pose a problem. You've been here a long time. What can you tell me about Link Stone?"

What was he doing? The last thing she wanted was to give Pam a heads-up, because then she'd call Grant or someone else, and then everything she was looking into, the links and the evidence, would suddenly disappear. She pressed her lips together and stared at Mark. He had to know what she was thinking.

"Link? What do you want to know about Link? You were asking about Link this morning, too, about a file of his. What's going on?"

Billy Jo put the loaded pizza back in the box and took in Lucky, who was lying on the other side of it, eyeing it. She uncrossed her legs, her feet bare, and stood up to toss the box on top of the file cabinet. "You know what, Pam? It's probably nothing, just a question I have, and…"

"So you're pulling all the files out? There's paper everywhere. You know I'm going to have to put this all back in the cabinet. I had it all organized."

Billy Jo didn't miss the fury directed her way. "You won't have to put anything away. I'll do it."

"I still need you to tell me about Link Stone,"

Mark said. "You worked with him, didn't you? Because there are discrepancies in his case files." He just wouldn't let it go.

Pam walked around her to her desk, where there was a stack of files, two open.

Mark lifted a check, the one to Deena Rae, holding it so Pam could see. "See here? This check was made out to a young girl, and then it was signed over to Link Stone. You haven't answered me."

Pam furrowed her brow. "Link was here a long time, a great guy, worked with a lot of kids. He made a real difference, you know," she said, looking at Billy Jo. Then she looked back to Mark and reached for the check he was holding.

Mark flipped it over and pointed to the other side. "See that it's signed over to Link Stone? Was this something he did?"

She gestured to the check. "Was it cashed?"

Billy Jo crossed her arms and took a step into the circle. "The check hasn't been cashed, but it was in an envelope addressed to Link, and the envelope was tucked inside a file. I mean, you're the one who knew him and handled the files. Did you put it in there, or did Link?"

She glanced between Billy Jo and Mark, then lifted her hands in the air and let them fall. "I have no idea. Link handled his own files. Sure, okay, that's strange, but Link is one of the good guys, and I'm starting to get the feeling you're trying to pin something on him or make him look bad. He did more for these kids than anyone. He went above and beyond when they needed something."

"Like what? What did he do that had him going above and beyond?" Billy Jo said. "Because what I'm seeing is a lot that doesn't add up. There are kids in these files from three months of age to fourteen, over forty kids just in the files we looked into. He had payments coming to these kids, a three-month-old, an eight-year-old, a thirteen-year-old. That makes no sense. And when I went into the system to look for these kids, I couldn't find any of them."

Pam frowned. Mark hadn't pulled his gaze from her. She reached for one of the files and lifted the paper to read it, then shook her head. "You know how it is, Billy Jo. These kids get shuffled around and off the island. Records get lost all the time…"

"So why is there a request from you for money for these kids—for camp, school supplies, clothing? I could go on."

Pam looked over to her and then back to one of the files. She could tell she was a little thrown as she shook her head. Billy Jo lifted a sheet of paper to show a requisition with Pam's signature on it, pointing right to it.

"Okay, that is my signature," she said. "You know I fill these out, and I do it for you too. There are all kinds of requests that have to be submitted on every kind of form. I can't remember all of them. I'm sure there is a simple and reasonable explanation."

Billy Jo swept her hands out. She could feel Mark watching her. "Then explain why Link Stone was having checks issued to all these kids. A few, sure, but a three-month-old? I mean, how does a three-month-old cash a check, or a seven-year-old, or a nine-year-old? Do they even have bank accounts? I would really like to see all these cashed checks and who cashed them. What are the chances of that?"

Pam was now staring straight at her. Her face paled, and Billy Jo saw she understood clearly what she was accusing Link Stone of. "I'm sure you're wrong, I can find out from accounting in the morning. I know Joy in finance. She'll be able to pull up the cashed checks and see. I'm sure it's just a simple error or something…"

Billy Jo could feel herself going to that place of wanting to argue.

"That would be helpful, Pam," Mark said, cutting in. "But, just to be clear, because of the seriousness of this issue, I'm going to ask you to enquire on all these files." He slid over to her the piece of paper with all the names of the files in question. "I want you to call about each of these kids. Just ask to see the last check cashed and who cashed it for each of these names."

She shot him a bugged-out expression. "That's a lot of names. You know, I remember a few here— Dillon, Cam, Lea, Janny…" She looked over to Billy Jo. "I really hope you're wrong here. There has to be a simple, reasonable explanation. Have you called Link Stone?"

Mark didn't pull his gaze from Pam. "He transferred to Wyoming, right?" he said, though Billy Jo knew he wasn't there.

"No, he's retired now. Thought you knew. He's down in San Antonio. Said it was just too hard, the work, the kids, the same old. He said there's a point where you just have to say you've done all you can do, and he was at that point."

Billy Jo wondered how close Pam was to Link. She sounded unusually fond of him. "You know where he is and how I could get a hold of him?"

Pam shrugged, opened the middle drawer of her desk, and pulled out a card. "He sends me a birthday card every year." She held up the card and the red envelope. "That's his address. Do you want his phone number?"

Mark took the envelope. "Yeah, give me his number—and in the meantime, Pam, I don't want you calling him. Call your friend in accounting and give me the information about who cashed those checks, and then I'll call Link Stone. You do not talk to anyone about this."

Even she could hear the warning in Mark's tone.

Pam lifted her hands and shook her head. "Understood. Call accounting. But, again, I know Link. He's one of the good ones. When you find out you're wrong, and you will, I hope he never learns how you, Billy Jo, and you, Chief, questioned his moral character." Then she slung her purse over her shoulder and narrowed her gaze at Billy Jo as she walked around her desk and started to the front door.

Then she turned back. "And you know what? I have enough to do when I come in in the morning, and the last thing I want to do is clean this up. So, with all due respect, I expect all these files to be neatly put back in the cabinet exactly the way I left them." Then she walked away to the door, pushed it open, and walked out.

Billy Jo listened to the key in the deadbolt, then dragged her gaze back to Mark, who had an odd look, still watching the door where Pam had walked out. When he looked over to her, she could see something she'd seen only a time or two.

"You think she'll call him and tell him we're looking?" he said. It was a good question and one she didn't know how to answer.

"I don't know. I hope she doesn't, but she could," she said. She looked over to Lucky, who had his eyes closed, tired, just like she should've been.

"Well, I think we've done all we can tonight," he said.

She knew he was right. "Why don't you head out? I'll put the files away and meet you at home."

Mark reached for one file and then another and stacked them on the desk. "Nope, I'm not leaving you here alone. I know how to file. You can double-check the names on the list and I'll put them away."

He shook his head again, and she could see the heavy thoughts lingering in the way his brow knit, the way he looked across the room as if thinking. He looked back to her. "You know, Billy Jo, I hope Pam is right."

"But you know she's not."

He let out a heavy sigh. "You know me too well,"

he said, then pulled open the drawer. "Come on, hand me those files."

She took a step over to him and ran her hand over his arm, his back. She leaned against him a second, letting her hand link with his. "I love you."

He leaned down and kissed the top of her head. "I know. I'm a catch."

She nudged his arm and couldn't hide the smile that only he could put there. "You really are arrogant."

He winked. "Yeah, I am—and yours."

Chapter 4

"Mark, coffee," Billy Jo said.

He stood under the spray of the shower, and Billy Jo poked her head in past the clear shower curtain. He was almost tempted to pull her into the shower with him, but she was holding out a mug of coffee, so he reached for it and stepped out of the spray to take a swallow, then leaned down and kissed her. He took another swallow before handing the mug back to her.

"You know, you could step out of those clothes and join me for some shower sex to start the day," he said.

She let her gaze linger on his chest and then lower, taking in all of him, and then back up as if she didn't have a shy bone in her body. "I had a shower, and now I'm dressed. That shower is a tiny box that's barely big enough for one."

She pulled the clear shower curtain back in place, and he could see her through it at the sink as she set his mug down and began brushing her teeth. Mark turned off the shower, pulled back the curtain, and reached for a faded gray towel on a hook to run over his chest and head.

"So let's get a bigger place," he said.

Billy Jo spit out the toothpaste, rinsed her mouth and toothbrush, tucked it in the holder, and reached for a hand towel to wipe her face before slowly turning to him. "You want to get a bigger place? I thought you liked this secluded hidden-away cabin of yours."

What was he supposed to say? It was a temporary place he'd found, but he'd been thinking of a lot more permanence as of late. "Would be kind of nice to have our own place. I'm now the chief. This is a small place, great for a single guy, but I'm not that anymore. Was thinking of a house on the island here, with three bedrooms, a big yard for Lucky, some bright windows for Harley to look out of…"

She didn't smile. She was pulling back into herself, and he wondered if she'd just walk out of the bathroom. He dried his legs and back, then looped the towel around his waist as she stood there, her arms now crossed. Then she did walk out.

He shut his eyes, hung his head. "Way to push there, Romeo," he muttered under his breath. He heard her in the kitchen as he reached for his toothbrush and turned on the tap.

"You know, Mark, I'm not scared, if that's what you're thinking."

He squeezed a good amount of toothpaste onto

his toothbrush. "You're terrified, and I'm tiptoeing around you. See? A second ago, you ran out."

She was leaning in the doorway now, and he let his gaze linger on her while he shoved the toothbrush in his mouth and started brushing. "I didn't run out. I stepped out because I needed to give myself a second to figure out what you're saying. You want a bigger place..."

He spit the toothpaste out and leaned down to the tap, where the water was running. He swished the water in his mouth and spit it out, then pulled his hand over his face to wipe it as he turned off the tap. "I want us to buy our own place, you know, a house, the kind that comes with setting down roots and eventually having a family."

She frowned. He could see her freaking out, and he hadn't even said the one thing he wanted to but knew he couldn't. "With me...?" He thought her voice squeaked.

"No, with Gail! For the love of God, Billy Jo, who else?" He brushed past her into the bedroom and tossed the towel onto the made bed, something else she had done. She was always up first, showered and dressed before he was even out of bed. Lazing around and waking up slowly together was something she didn't do.

He pulled open the top drawer of the dresser, seeing her underwear and socks next to his. He pulled out his black boxer briefs and stepped into them, and he knew she was still there behind him, watching and saying nothing. There were times, like now, that he wanted to shake her, and he would if he thought it would do any good. He pulled open the bottom drawer and reached for a clean pair of jeans, seeing how neatly everything was folded in the drawers now.

"Okay."

He still had his back to her, stepping into his jeans and zipping them up. He turned to her. For a second, he didn't think he'd heard her right. "You said yes?"

Her arms were crossed, and he could see she really was struggling, scared, but she wasn't letting herself run. She nodded. "Harley would like a big picture window with a lot of morning sun, Lucky deserves a big yard, and I'd like to have a kitchen with a dishwasher and counter space."

He didn't know what to say. "I'll call a realtor, get the ball rolling. Any other requests?"

She uncrossed her arms. Her navy T-shirt was flattering and simple, and her black capris were so her. She took a step over to him and then another, then ran her hand over his arm, the discoloration of where the tattoo had once been. He was glad it was gone, but he was thinking of another tattoo now, on his other arm—something that wasn't the face of a girl.

"I was thinking about this morning," she said. "While you talk to Pam about the accounting and the checks, I'm going to do some digging on each of these kids, find out where they are and a little bit about their situations, you know, put it together. You're going to the station first?"

So that was it. All talk of the house was gone. But then, when something made Billy Jo uncomfortable, like their evolving relationship, she shut down. At least she was still there.

"I'll call Lacy," he said. "I think after last night, I'll follow you in and catch Pam early to make sure she looks into what I asked her to."

Billy Jo let her hand linger on his bare arm. Then her fingers traced down and over to his chest. She stepped in closer and rose up on her tiptoes, where he met her halfway and kissed her, letting it linger a second before she pulled back and started walking, gesturing to the bathroom.

"Don't forget your coffee," she said. "It's probably already cold. You want me to top it up?" She glanced back to him.

"Sure, thanks." Mark opened the middle drawer and reached for a navy T-shirt to pull over his head.

"You know, Mark, I would also like a double wall oven, a gas cooktop, and an island in the kitchen. I don't need an ocean view, but a quiet property would be best, where we can't see or hear the neighbors."

He looked over to her where she was holding his mug. He hadn't expected that from her, and he couldn't help the easy smile that touched his lips. "You got it."

She walked out of the bedroom, into the kitchen of his small cabin, and he watched as she poured him a coffee. His dog brushed up to her, and she smiled brightly to him and bent over, making a big fuss. He wondered if this was how his brothers had felt before deciding to ask their wives to marry them.

"Okay, slow down, Mark," he said to himself.

"Did you say something?" Billy Jo called out.

He shook his head, taking in his image in the mirror. "Just pour the coffee in two go-mugs," he said. "I'll have some cereal, and then let's get going." He pulled out a pair of socks and couldn't help thinking of a ring on her finger, something simple and small.

She lifted her cat and carried him, and whatever she was saying to him, he wondered whether she had any idea of what he was thinking of doing.

"Baby steps there, Mark," he said in a lower voice now, watching his girl, who was starting to come around.

But he could move only so fast, because there was one thing he knew about Billy Jo: He needed to give her enough time to get used to an idea. He thought of that ring again, wondering when he could finally ask her and when she'd finally be ready to say yes.

Chapter 5

Billy Jo could hear Mark talking to Pam, but whatever he was saying to her, she couldn't make it out. She typed another name from the long list into the computer for the CPS system, then reached for the phone again to dial the number of a facility called the Braxton Institute. She listened to the ring, and then she heard a buzz and an automated message: "This number is not in service."

She took in the list of places the children apparently were. So far, she had discovered exactly the same thing for each: no number in service.

"The Braxton Institute, Coronaldi, Pleaseman Detention Center, and a numbered company, 567899… Like, what the hell is all this?" she said, staring at the names. An icy unsettled feeling lingered inside her. Where were the names of the families the kids should have been placed with?

She pushed back her chair, holding the paper, and walked out of her office to see Mark standing in front of Pam's desk, reading something from a file, while Pam was on the phone. Mark looked right at her as she walked over, and just the way he was watching her, she realized how much she depended on him. He was her go-to, her person to lean on, and she didn't know what she'd do if he weren't there.

"What's wrong?" he said. That was just something else that was too perfect about him. He could read her so well.

"I can't find these kids. I've made it halfway through the list, and all that's come up has been a detention center, an institution, a numbered company… I've never heard of any of these places, Mark. I called two of them, and I keep getting a number not in service message. For the numbered company, there's no phone number at all, and I can't find anything about it or where it is." She held the sheet of paper out to him, and he took it from her.

Pam hung up the phone and turned to her. "That was Grant. He's coming out to the island because of the issue with Link's files."

"You called Grant and told him?" She knew she sounded accusing, but Pam shook her head.

"He called me. Apparently, Joy from accounting called him to give him a heads-up after I called about those checks. Several were cashed by Link Stone, but how or why, I don't know," Pam said, then lifted her hands.

Billy Jo dragged her gaze over to Mark, whose expression was all cop. "You tell Joy I want a copy of all the checks cashed by Link Stone, all of them," he said. "For every payment issued to kids on this list, I need to know what it was supposed to be for and where it was sent. I want to know who cashed them."

Pam just stared at Mark, then looked over to Billy Jo.

"Pam, these kids were sent to places I've never heard of before," Billy Jo said, reaching for the paper Mark was still looking at. He dragged his gaze to her and let her take it back, and she put it on the desk in front of Pam. "Have you ever heard of these places? Because I haven't." Her finger was on the paper by the names, and the odd look on Pam's face said everything.

Pam shook her head and looked up to her. "No, I haven't. Where are these places? Are you sure that's right? All the kids?"

Billy Jo turned to Mark, who was watching Pam and her. He held his hand out for the paper again and said, "I'll give this to Elisha, get her to check it out. She was looking into Link, as well. I think it's time I have a talk with him and find out what this is, see what light he can shed on it."

Pam said nothing, just linked her fingers, clasping them in front of her. Her demeanour gave Billy Jo an off feeling. Finally, she said, "I called him last night. I'm sorry, but Link is a friend, and I've known him for a long time. I can't believe he would do something like this. There has to be another explanation, and—"

"Pam, Mark told you very clearly not to call him," Billy Jo snapped, cutting her off.

"I know what you said, but I know Link, and

there's no way he's good for this. He has to have been set up. There's no other explanation!" Pam yelled, ready to fight back.

"Hey, enough. Stop this," Mark said, shaking his head. "Pam, I was clear when I told you not to say anything to Link."

Billy Jo had to pull her hands over her chest and squeeze her forearms to resist the urge to wrap them around Pam's throat.

"So please tell me what his explanation was," Mark continued, and she didn't know how he could sound so calm. "I take it he denied it."

Pam turned to Billy Jo without pulling her gaze from Mark, and she wondered whether she was trying to figure out what not to say.

"Pam, so help me God, if you lie or hold anything back…"

"Oh, hush up!" Pam snapped at her, and Billy Jo had to take a step back. She couldn't remember ever being on this end of such nastiness from Pam before. "Link Stone is one of the finest men I know. He remembered every birthday I ever had. He was the one there for me when my husband cheated on me. We worked it out, likely because of Link and what a good friend he was to me. I watched how he cared for those kids, every one of them, wishing he could do more. I know his kids, too, and was at their birthdays, graduations… We barbecued on weekends. There's no way he's good for this." She really was on the defensive.

"So he said it wasn't true?" Mark cut in.

Pam shook her head. "He was thrown, likely because I woke him in the middle of the night. He was real quiet on the phone. He was upset. I could hear it in his voice."

Mark was watching Pam as a cop would. She'd seen this side of him so many times with people. "And what, exactly, did Link say? Did he say he didn't do it, Pam?"

Again, she shook her head. "No, he didn't come right out and say he didn't do it. He said he'd call me back."

Billy Jo realized she was fisting her hands, staring at Pam, wondering how she couldn't get through to her.

Pam glanced over at Billy Jo. "And don't look at me like that. If you were in my position and someone accused Mark of something heinous, even if there was evidence that pointed at him, you can't honestly tell me you would just believe it," she said, fire flickering in her eyes.

Billy Jo wondered if she hissed as she stepped back. She made herself look over to Mark as if he could make sense of this, then said, "Well, first, Pam, Mark wouldn't do something like this. He wouldn't cash checks made out to kids and then try to hide it, so don't you dare turn this on me and the man I love. I hate to tell you this, but a bunch of kids are missing. On first glance, it seems they've vanished, yet these checks were issued to them. How many were cashed by Link Stone? He didn't deny it and said he'd call you back, but I'll tell you why he got off the phone—

because he's trying to figure out how the hell to cover his tracks. You just tipped off a man who was responsible for these children and needed to do right by them. How the hell do you explain any of this?" She couldn't remember ever yelling at Pam, at anyone, like this.

"Billy Jo," Mark said in that calm voice. He stepped over to her and ran his hand over her back. His touch usually settled her, but right now she was too furious with a woman who'd chosen to protect a man she knew deep down was responsible in some way for something she had a bad feeling about.

"You deal with her," Billy Jo said. "I'm going to see what I can find out about these kids, where they came from, their parents, anything."

He slid his hand over her cheek, the touch gentle, and she took the paper from Pam and rested her hand on Mark's chest before walking past and back to her office. She heard Mark say to her, "Okay, Pam, get Link on the phone, because right now, I want to have a word with him."

Billy Jo glanced back to Mark, who she had to remind herself was now the chief on the island, the man she loved. She had this awful unsettled feeling she'd never felt before.

She squeezed the paper and looked at the names of the kids, the ages she'd written beside them, and the places they supposedly were, and she walked over to her desk and pushed the laptop back. She hesitated only a second before lifting the phone and dialing home.

It rang only once before she heard, "Chase McCabe." The way he said it, she knew he was distracted, evidently working.

"Hi, Dad, you got a minute?"

"Hey, sweetheart, always for you. What's up?"

"Well, a few things I need your help with. I wonder if I can run something past you." She heard something in the background.

"You know you can ask anything, right?" he said.

She wondered when she would tell him how serious it was with Mark. She leaned back in her chair and stared at the names of the kids, the places they were supposed to be. "Yeah, I know. I've hit a brick wall on something. If I send you the names of some businesses, some institutions kids were sent to... I can't find anything about them, and the numbers I called were not in service. It just feels off."

"And you're not talking to Mark about this?"

There it was, the curiosity. "He's here now, and yes, he's also helping."

"Well, that's good," Chase said. "You don't have to explain. Send me the names, and I'll do some digging, make some calls, and see what I can turn up. Anything else you want to tell me about you and Mark?"

Why did it seem as if he knew something?

"We're going house-hunting, you know, getting a bigger place," she said. Her dad was quiet, and for a second, she wasn't sure he was still there. "Dad?"

"Yeah, sorry. I thought you said you and Mark are house-hunting."

She knew her dad was teasing. "Okay, stop it. Yes, we're still together, and I did say that. Now, how about I send those company names and you let me know what you can find? Oh, and one more thing! Dad, remember Carmen Zarko, who took over as detective? Well, she found herself on a no-fly list, some bureaucratic mistake that has her listed as a person of interest. I told Mark I'd call you…"

Her dad sighed on the other end. "Send it my way, darling. You know I'll do what I can. Hey, and, Billy Jo?"

She was leaning back in her chair, squeezing the phone, knowing her dad was likely going to toss out unwanted advice, so she said nothing.

Instead, he said, "It's really nice to hear you're so happy."

She hadn't expected that. "Thanks, Dad," she replied.

Then she hung up and stared at the phone, the paper, and her laptop, for a moment wishing that just once, something good could happen for these kids, as it seemed nothing ever went their way.

Chapter 6

Mark tapped on Billy Jo's office door, taking in the woman who meant everything to him. She was scrolling through something on her laptop, sitting in her chair, one hand squeezing her chin. She looked over to him.

"I need to head out to the station," he said. "You going to be okay here?" When he spotted Lucky curled up on the sofa, the dog lifted his head but didn't jump down.

"Why wouldn't I be?" Billy Jo said with an edge in her voice. She slid around in her chair and let out a heavy sigh, then linked her hands over the flat of her stomach, not pulling her gaze from him, unsettled.

"Oh, I don't know. With the way you went at Pam out there, I just wanted to make sure I didn't leave here only to have to respond to a 911 because you've killed her."

She narrowed her gaze. The way her mouth tightened, he could see she wasn't amused in the least.

"Seriously?" She shook her head. "Doesn't dignify an answer, Mark. What about Link? You talked to him? Please tell me how he explained this away, because I want that prick sitting in front of me so I can demand he answer to everything he did. I want him to look me in the eye and tell me he wasn't screwing over those kids."

He knew he couldn't hide any of this from Billy Jo. "Didn't talk to him. Had Pam call, but it went to voicemail. Made her try again, but still voicemail, so the last time I made it official and told him to call back the chief of police." He couldn't shake the feeling that Pam had warned the guy off, calling him to give him a heads-up.

"You think he knows?" Billy Jo said.

Mark stepped into the small office and sat at the edge of her desk, taking in her open laptop, the files. She was so close he could feel her. "I think I don't really know what's going on between Pam and Link, but something's off. Maybe he's not picking up because she warned him, or maybe there's something else. It could be completely innocent. I don't know anything other than the fact that some checks were cashed and Link has a lot to explain.

"You know, I wish Carmen were here right now, but she's not, so I'll get Elisha to look into all the details of the checks. I asked Pam to review every case Link had and find out why he requested money for those kids. What was it for? She'll pull every one of his cases, everything ever assigned to him. Who knows how many more kids there were? I'll ask Elisha to get access to his bank account, too, and I'll put a call in to the DA and get a court order to make it all legal if I have to. You find out anything?"

She looked back to her laptop and then tapped the keyboard. "I called my dad. One, he'll look into the Carmen situation and see what he can do. Two, I sent him the list of institutions where the kids are supposed to be, the ones I can't contact, and he's going to see what he can find. Mark, I have a really bad feeling. It shouldn't be this difficult to find kids. When CPS pulls them, they go to a family, and it's in the file, and there's a phone number, a person you can call. There are group homes, too. And I hate to say this, but lastly, when anyone has a problem with a kid, they can stick them into a locked facility, a jail, but you still know where they are. Why can't I find anything?"

He heard a male voice and frowned at the way Billy Jo stiffened, looking at the door, before she pushed back her chair.

"That would be Grant," she said. She pressed both hands to the arms of the chair and stood up, and Mark followed her out into the hall to see a man of average height, soft in the middle, wearing a navy dress shirt, slacks, and glasses, balding on top, holding a jacket over his arm and a briefcase. He was talking to Pam, and then he dragged his gaze over to Billy Jo and to Mark, who was right behind her.

"I know both of you have questions about some payments and checks," he began, "but before anyone goes too far down the rabbit hole of conspiracy here, this is how it's going to play out. The agency has a clear position on issues like this, with a process that has to be followed. Jumping to conclusions isn't going to happen. We're going to slow down and walk back whatever this is. Link will be contacted, but no one is talking to anyone outside of this agency."

Mark didn't have to look at Billy Jo's face to know she wasn't taking this lying down. She stiffened as Grant looked over to him and said, "You must be Chief Friessen."

Mark held out his hand. "I am. Nice to put a face to the name."

For a moment, he didn't think Grant would shake his hand, but he did—a little softly, he thought. He could already see the man didn't want to give him anything. Just what the hell was going on?

"Pam," Grant said, "you are not to give anything else to Chief Friessen. From this point forward, Chief, I'm going to ask you to leave the office, because there's nothing official going on here."

That was not what he'd been expecting.

"Now just hang on a second, Grant," Billy Jo said. "There are signs of impropriety, a government official taking money from a minor, so this is now a police matter, and Mark has every right to be here. In fact, I insist he be here. Checks have been issued to kids with no explanation and then signed over to Link Stone. Did you know about this? Then there's the matter of my not being able to find the kids. These institutions, I can't find anything on them. I called two, and the numbers are not in service."

He could hear the fight in her, but he knew when a government agency was circling the wagons. God damn, he didn't want to be right about this.

Grant dragged his gaze from Billy Jo to Pam and back. "You forget you work for the state, Billy Jo?" he said. "If your boss tells you to put away a file, you put it away. It's more than likely that this is a clerical error someplace, as simple as that. Before an alarm is sounded, everyone is going to take a minute. You're going to take a minute. There are procedures in place and oversight to prevent something like this from happening.

"Joy will not be sending any documents to you, Chief Friessen, from what I understand and the phone call from Pam, and from this point forward, nothing else will be forthcoming on Link Stone. He's retired. Any discussions will have to go through our legal department. You can submit a document request, but it takes time to process. You have active cases, Billy Jo, and one is the Gillespie file. Word has come down you'll have to find a new placement for those kids, so you need to handle that today."

The boss was shutting down Billy Jo and forcing her hand, but he knew his girl couldn't be told what she had to walk away from.

"Excuse me, Grant. Can I have a word?" Mark said. He reached over to Billy Jo and touched her arm, feeling how tight she was, not ready to back down. She wasn't a woman who could be handled, and she didn't pull her fiery gaze from Grant, wanting to argue, to fight. Then she did, instead looking up to him with that kill or be killed look he knew all too well.

"You know what, Chief? I'm not sure I can be any more clear…"

Mark took a step in front of Billy Jo, then another until he was standing right in front of Grant, and the man took a step back, unnerved, looking up at him. But he seemed suddenly ready to stand his ground.

"You are supposed to be on the side of innocent kids," Mark said, "but this is beginning to sound like you're all about protecting your agency. Link worked here for how long? For how many kids was he the social worker of record? How many kids did he request money for, checks, and how many of those were signed over to him? I will find out. I'll get a warrant if I have to."

"Then you do that, Chief," Grant said, nearly cutting him off, challenging him with arrogance. "But don't come in here expecting to see confidential files you do not have the legal authority to access. I'm going to ask you to leave, Chief Friessen, and if you refuse, I will contact my supervisor, who will contact your boss, and then let's see who wins here. I guarantee it won't be you. Now good day, Chief."

With that dismissal, Grant walked around him and dumped his jacket and briefcase on Pam's desk. Pam appeared so damn uncomfortable, but Billy Jo was another story, staring daggers at Grant. He knew she might very well be walked out of there, as she was not a woman who would ever go quietly into the night.

"I'll call you later," he said to her. Then, instead of walking to where Grant now stood with the door open, he strode over to Billy Jo and leaned down and kissed her. When he pulled back, he let his thumbs brush her cheeks. "Don't worry. Do what you have to do here. I'll do some digging on my end. This isn't forgotten or buried."

She wrapped her hands around his wrists, pulled her lower lip between her teeth, and then nodded. "Call if you find anything."

He let his hands fall away. "Lucky, come on, boy," he called out, then whistled for the dog, who trotted out of Billy Jo's office and started walking to the door, where Grant was still standing, waiting to toss him out. He knew from how unimpressed he seemed that he'd seen the kiss and figured out the personal relationship between him and Billy Jo.

Lucky was already outside when Mark reached the door and said in a low voice, "Just to be clear, messing with Billy Jo means messing with me, and I'm not someone you want to mess with, Grant." He tapped the back of his hand to Grant's chest, not even trying to hide the warning.

"You threatening me, Chief Friessen? Because that sounded like you issuing a threat to a public official."

He really was a piece of work.

"Oh, I don't threaten people," Mark said.

Grant didn't look away. "Good luck getting your warrant."

Maybe it was the way he said it, but Mark had a

feeling the evidence Billy Jo had found could quickly disappear. He glanced back once to the women, who were watching them, and then he stepped out. The door pulled closed behind him, and he heard the lock click.

He took in his dog waiting in front of his Jeep.

Damn! He hadn't wanted this to be true, but he'd never seen something shut down so quickly. The thing he feared was that a bunch of kids, kids whose welfare should have been the only concern of Grant and CPS, were being ignored.

Kids and animals… That you never messed with either, or so help you God, was a code Mark lived and breathed.

Chapter 7

She had never hated Grant as much as she did now, when he was yanking at the leash he had suddenly strung around her neck, making some fucking statement about how he could do whatever he wanted to her and she could do nothing.

But he was wrong. He didn't know anything about who she was and what she'd survived as a kid. It hadn't broken her. Instead, it had made her ready to fight and come out swinging. Billy Jo McCabe would never just go along with something or look away because she'd been told to. Maybe some did, but she was a fighter.

At the same time, it took everything she had inside her to sit where she was and do nothing for now, because she'd learned never to take on a fight until she was ready.

Where was Grant now but in her office? He'd taken it over, and she had once again been relegated to a desk in a cubicle. Pam was still at the front, at her desk, and had said nothing else to her. She wondered if the glare she continued to toss her way was why she was refusing to look at her.

"I'm still waiting on the Baker report," Grant called out. "And I told you to move those Gillespie kids."

She stood, looking over at Grant, feeling how he was deliberately trying to control her time and what she did. She'd never have believed Grant could know something about this mess of Link's, but right now she was seeing a man she realized she hadn't known at all.

"The Baker report was emailed to you," she said. "The Gillespie kids are Erin and Kai, sisters, eight and ten, whom I have no intention of breaking up. I have an appointment tomorrow with the Fitzpatricks, who have them, to sit down and sort out the issue."

"I told you to move them, not negotiate. That's what came in. You don't have the luxury of keeping them together. Your only job is to put them someplace else, and if you're not going to do your job, I'll get someone else to do it."

She had to remind herself that he was her boss and she had to listen to him, but she had no intention of splitting up sisters who had only each other. She pulled her arms over her chest and looked away, willing herself to come up with something intelligent to say as she shook her head. "I'm not separating those girls."

Grant neither nodded nor looked away from her. "Pam," he said, "I want you to call the Fitzpatricks and tell them I'm on my way over to pick up the girls. Find me an emergency placement for them tonight."

Billy Jo felt her mouth gape. "What are you doing? I said I would handle it. That's my case."

"Not anymore, it's not. You seem to be overstepping a lot here, Billy Jo. Your job as a social worker isn't to think for yourself; it's to follow orders, and you can't seem to do that. I think you should take some time off, a few days, and when you get your head screwed on straight, you and I'll sit down and have a talk on where we go from here. I'm thinking your priorities may have become a little skewed, considering your relationship with the chief. Maybe you've had too much free rein on how to handle things. Let me ask you, how much information have you shared with him about files you don't have the authority to share?"

She knew Pam was listening, and she could feel herself being walked to the door. "With all due respect, Grant, my personal relationship with Mark is not your business, and anything I share with Mark isn't a secret. You're well aware of the policy that was implemented on this island, which means the chief is notified anytime a child is taken from a home so he's aware of what's going on in the community. Have I missed something? Are the police here no longer meant to work with social services? Because I know you were notified of this."

Damn, she was proud of herself. She couldn't remember ever having seen the pissed-off expression Grant wore now.

He shook his head and gestured quite sharply to the door. "Go now. You're off for a week. Get your things and go."

Wow, the nastiness was there. She wanted to stay and argue, but she couldn't, not with the way he was coming at her. She could almost hear Mark and her dad telling her to stand down, walk away, so she let out a rough sigh, reached for her sweater on the back of the chair, and pulled it on. Then she reached for her bag on the floor and her laptop.

"You can leave the computer," Grant said. "Anything that belongs to the state stays. Just take yourself, not a pen, a paper, a file, or anything that belongs to the agency."

She didn't put the laptop down. Instead, she lifted it to show him before tucking it into her big purse. "This laptop isn't owned by CPS. This was a gift from my dad, so no, you're not keeping it. The cheap laptop owned by CPS is still in its original box on the shelf beside the file cabinet. If you ask Pam, I'm sure she'll show you."

She lifted her bag over her shoulder and started past Grant, seeing Pam's wide eyes and pale face, but she said nothing. Billy Jo walked right to the front door and flicked the lock. She didn't have to turn to know Grant was right behind her. She could feel his energy, his anger.

"Key, too," he said, holding his hand out, and she realized he was serious.

"You want my key to the building? Thought I was just taking a few days off. You firing me now?"

His expression was hard, unforgiving, and his hand was still out. He said nothing. There was a point where this could turn really ugly, so she pulled her keys from inside her purse and worked the office key from the ring, then held it up, not giving it to him.

"Are you firing me, Grant, yes or no? Because with you asking for the key and taking this hard line, it sounds to me like I've stepped into something you don't want me looking too closely at or asking questions about. Let me ask you, Grant, did you know about those checks, those kids? How many are there? What else are you hiding?"

He reached for the key and ripped it from her hand.

"Wow, really?" she snapped. "You know what, Grant? You may be able to toss me out, but now I know you're trying to bury something. Why is what I don't know. How deep does this go, Grant, the money, the checks? What's really going on? Don't want to answer me? Fine, don't answer, but Mark isn't going to let this go, and he's good at what he does. And I'm going to help him, because I won't be silenced. You may be able to lock me out of here, but I know you can't hide everything. I will uncover what you did, what Link did, and so help me, Grant, if you did something illegal, I will make it my personal mission to see you behind bars, you and everyone involved, anyone who looked away, knowing something very wrong was happening, and said nothing." Her heart thudded long and loud in her ears.

"You're done," he said. "Out, now."

He took a step closer to her, forcing her out the door, and she stood out on the sidewalk, furious, trembling inside. He said nothing else, just pulled the door closed and locked it.

He was hiding something, but all she could think of were the Gillespie girls. Because she hadn't toed the line, she realized those girls were going to be separated.

"Fuck!" She kicked the door, hearing the rattle.

Why did it seem she was damned if she did and damned if she didn't? But whatever was going on, she had no intention of keeping her nose out of what Grant was hiding—and he was hiding something, about Link Stone, about the checks.

"Grant, I will see you in hell for whatever you have your hand in," she said in a low voice even though she knew he wouldn't hear it.

Then she walked over to her car and slid in behind the wheel. She could just make out Pam and Grant talking through the tinted window, looking her way. Whatever they were talking about, she realized someone evidently didn't want the truth to come out.

Yes, she knew they were hiding something.

Chapter 8

"Look, I have a copy of the check that was signed over to Link Stone," Mark said. "A lot of checks were made out to several kids Link was looking after, some issued every month for years, and he cashed them after they were signed over to him. There's the question of whose signature is really on the backs of those checks…"

"You don't have the evidence, and CPS has already come back to say that information was obtained without a warrant. They're saying they're currently looking into it as a clerical error," said Assistant DA Cole Mitchell over the phone. He was another new face; it seemed assistant DAs went through a revolving door every few years. He was young, light haired, and had always worn a suit the few times Mark had been face to face with him.

"Look, these are the most vulnerable kids," Mark said. "We need the warrant to get access to his records. This social worker is having kids sign over checks and cashing them. Doesn't that seem a little odd to you? Clerical error, my ass. This is them scrubbing their records and shredding anything so we can't find the truth. And it's not as if some of these kids would even know how to sign over a check, considering how young they were. One in particular was only three months. And now we can't find these kids. The social worker on the case—"

"You mean Billy Jo McCabe, your girlfriend," Cole cut in before he could finish.

At a tap on his door, Mark swung around his chair. Elisha stood there, holding up a file, dimples popping in the dark skin of her plump round cheeks.

He gestured for her to come in. "Look, my relationship with Billy Jo is irrelevant…"

"Well, I disagree, and so does CPS, considering they're saying she didn't have the authority to involve you, so this was basically a girlfriend showing her boyfriend confidential files."

He sat forward in his chair as he heard the door to the precinct opening, and he looked around Elisha, who was standing in front of his desk, to see Billy Jo walking in. "Look, Cole, don't you see what this is? They're covering their asses because they know a social worker did something and it's going to look really bad. I don't know what we're looking at, fraud, criminal conspiracy…"

"I hear you, Mark, and I'm empathetic, but if you want something to stick, you need to get something I can use to go to a judge, something that has real teeth, like a smoking gun. Unfortunately, what you have now is an uncashed check stuck in a file, which could have been stuck there by anyone, and an uncashed check in a file isn't evidence of anything. Get me something solid, and I'll get you a warrant.

"Chief, word of advice? If your relationship with Ms. McCabe is being used as a reason not to look into this, then you've stepped on some toes. You don't have copies of all those checks you said were cashed, and your conversation over the phone with someone from the accounting department is now being disputed. Make sure everything you get from now on is solid, and then come back to me with something more. A statement from the kids would be helpful."

Then ADA Mitchell hung up, and Mark set the phone back in the cradle and lifted his gaze to both Billy Jo and Elisha.

"So what did you find?" he said to Elisha, who handed him a file.

"You were asking about Link Stone," she said. "He owns a house in San Antonio, a really nice house worth more than I would ever be able to afford. From the tax records, it cost him 1.98 million."

Mark took the file and was now leaning forward, Billy Jo dragging her gaze from him to Elisha. "That's quite a house on a social worker's salary," he said.

"Well, he could have had some good investments," Elisha said, then shrugged, and he wondered if she was serious. He was still trying to figure her out. "But you may be interested to know that before Link Stone was a social worker here for eight years, he did five in Seattle and four in Spokane, and before that he was out in Minnesota. Interestingly enough, he was in St. Paul, which is my hometown, and my cousin works in the sheriff's department there.

"So I made a call, and it seems there were questions during his time about unaccounted money involving kids he was the social worker of record for. A teenager filed an accusation against him, saying he was taking her checks. My cousin said he remembered it because the girl was loud and adamant, but she was still in the care of the state. CPS said it had been an accounting error, and the girl in question had a history with authority and was a compulsive liar. They ran their own internal investigation."

Billy Jo had an odd look on her face and was watching Elisha intently. "Let me guess. Their investigation went nowhere, and the matter died a slow quiet death and was filed away."

Elisha pulled her arms over her chest and shrugged. "Pretty much what he said. I know it's not a lot to go on, but I did ask him for the name of the girl in case you want to talk to her."

Billy Jo was looking at Elisha with the same expression Mark was. His newest deputy had surprised the hell out of him.

"Yeah, give me everything," he said.

She gestured toward the file. "It's in there. Kristi Moore is her name, but I don't have a number for her or her whereabouts, and this was a long time ago now, so I don't know if she's still in St. Paul."

"Find her," Mark said. Billy Jo rested her bag with

her laptop sticking out on a chair and let out a sigh. He could see how off she was.

"I'll start looking," Elisha said. "Oh, and the number you gave me for Link Stone was his cell phone, so his home number is now in the file as well. He has a wife, Melinda, and two daughters, Lynn and Bev. One is currently at Stanford, and the other graduated Harvard with a bachelor of science and is getting married next month. She's posted all over social media because the wedding will be a social event at a golf club where her father is a member, and the guest list is massive. In other words, a retired social worker's salary isn't going to pay for all that, so either he won the lottery, or…"

Mark had a sick feeling, and Billy Jo was looking away from him, seething in a way he'd never seen before. "Okay, thanks, Elisha. Let me know whatever else you find, and track down Kristi Moore. Close the door behind you," he said. Elisha walked out of his office, and Billy Jo was now staring long and hard at him, her arms pulled over her chest. "You want to tell me what's going on? Because it's written all over your face."

The fire in her eyes flickered, and for a moment he wasn't sure she would say anything. "Grant basically fired my ass after we got into it. He said I was taking a few days off, which turned into me handing over my key and getting out. He's neck deep in this. I'd bet my bottom dollar. I couldn't keep it together and not challenge him, so the worst thing is that I've basically screwed over two little girls, sisters, whom he's going to pull from their home and separate." She let out a heavy sigh.

A weight settled on his shoulders. Damn, that asshole had messed with his girl, exactly what he'd warned him not to do. "Well, you can't do anything about the girls right now, but you can fix it when you get back in there. And you will. I'll give Link a call. Let's see what he has to say."

She leaned on his desk and flicked her gaze down to the open file, then turned it around to read everything on Link Stone. "I know you're right, but it doesn't make me feel any better. Well, come on, pick up the phone and call him." She pointed at the number in the file.

He put it on speaker and dialed as he sat forward in his chair. Billy Jo was sitting on the edge of his desk, looking intently between the phone and him as he listened to it ring once, then a second time before a woman said, "Hello?"

But something was off in her voice.

"Hello. This is Chief Mark Friessen from the Roche Harbor Police. I'm trying to get a hold of Link Stone."

"I'm Link's wife. Who did you say this was?" She sniffed loudly.

"I'm the chief of police in Roche Harbor. Your husband used to work on the island as a social worker, and some questions have come up about a case he was handling. Could I speak with him? This is quite important."

She said nothing for a second. "I'm sorry, that's not possible."

Billy Jo frowned and gestured to him, furious. He didn't like being jerked around, either. He knew she'd likely step in and say something, so he continued quickly.

"I'm sorry," he said, "but this is a police matter. I do need to speak with him. I've left two messages on his cell phone."

"You don't understand," the woman said. "It's not possible because he's dead."

Chapter 9

Billy Jo knew she was pacing in circles, so she stopped. Mark appeared far too calm as he stood and stared down at the phone he'd just settled back in the cradle. He leaned with both hands on his desk and then walked around her, his hand on her arm. She couldn't shake the feeling that a secret was being taken to the grave.

Mark pulled open the door and strode out of the office. "Elisha, I just got off the phone with Link Stone's wife. She said he's dead. I need you to call San Antonio and find out if this is true, and if it is, I want to know what happened."

The young deputy sitting at Carmen's old desk nodded and picked up the phone immediately, and Mark walked back into his office and dragged his hand over his face.

"Do you think she was lying?" was all Billy Jo could think to ask.

He shook his head and made a face, as thrown as

she was. "I don't know…" was all he got out before Elisha hung up the phone and called out, "Chief!"

Billy Jo heard her chair squeak back. Mark stepped out of his office, and she followed him.

"Link Stone hanged himself," Elisha said, meeting them halfway. "His wife found him."

"How did you find out so quickly? That was unbelievably fast."

She gestured to her desk. "I hadn't even finished calling the San Antonio PD. I pulled it up on the computer, and it was there in a news article, just posted."

Mark let out a heavy sigh. "Call San Antonio PD, find out who's handling the case, and get them on the phone for me right now."

"You got it, Chief," Elisha said before striding back to her desk. Billy Jo watched as Lacy, the new dispatcher, glanced up from Gail's old desk over to her. Mark pulled his hand over his face again.

"Suicide, really?" Billy Jo said as they walked back into his office. "That's not a coincidence, Mark. What the hell is going on?"

He shook his head, stepped around his desk, and perched on the edge. She could see he was thinking as he flicked those baby blues over to her. "No, I agree it sounds rather convenient. Let's see. Pam called him, and we have no idea what she said, but whatever it was, he then hanged himself instead of talking to us."

"Chief, I have a Detective Murphy on line two for you," Elisha called out. Billy Jo glanced at the young deputy through the office window as Mark reached for the phone and picked it up.

"Mark, put it on speaker," she said, then closed the door.

"This is Chief Mark Friessen," he said. "Is this Detective Murphy?"

"Yes, Chief. I was speaking with your deputy, and she indicated you're calling about Link Stone, a suicide."

Billy Jo pulled her arms tight across her chest, just staring at the phone, listening to the deep voice on the other end.

Mark shook his head. "I am. I'm wondering if you can tell me when this happened and what the circumstances were. I'm investigating a case up here, and Link Stone is a witness, so this leaves me with a lot of questions."

"That's really unfortunate. All I can tell you is his wife said he didn't come to bed last night, that he was upset because of a call or something. He wouldn't tell her what the problem was and said everything would be fine, but when she got up in the morning, she found him in the garage, where he'd hanged himself. She was incoherent when we arrived. He'd left a note that just said he was sorry."

Mark glanced up and made a face. "That's all there was, just a note, and that's all it said?"

He was sorry? Billy Jo shook her head. All she could think of was the kids, wondering what the hell he had done.

"Maybe you can shed some light on this for us,"

Murphy said. "When we asked his wife what it meant, she said she didn't know. We figured it was something between them, a fight, an argument, an affair he'd had, maybe one of those situations where the wife finds out. But you were investigating something. Would he have taken his own life over it?"

Mark was looking right at her, resting a hand on his thigh where he sat at the edge of the desk. "Link Stone was a social worker on my island, and there were some discrepancies in the files he was assigned to. We needed him to clear up some questions regarding payments he received. Listen, you wouldn't by any chance have access to his bank accounts, would you? Because I can tell you that him committing suicide only has us further questioning his involvement. He was in charge of some innocent kids. The house he owns down there, I understand he purchased it for 1.98 million?"

Billy Jo heard paper flipping in the background on the other end.

"We never looked into that," Murphy said. "We didn't see any signs of foul play, and because it was a suicide, I was about to close the file up. There were no signs of a struggle, and the ME has already ruled it a suicide by hanging. Should I be looking for something else?"

Billy Jo wasn't sure what to make of the way Mark was watching her. "Yeah," he said. "Can you get his financial records? And if it's all the same to you, Detective, I'm flying down there, and I'll come by and see you if you could make some time for me."

There was silence for a second. "Sure, I'll let my captain know. You'll be informing us of what it is you're investigating, what he was involved in?"

Billy Jo wasn't sure she wanted this detective knowing what she believed Link had done, or their investigation could get shut down again.

"Of course I will. I'll call you when we land," Mark said, then pressed the end button and flicked his all-cop gaze over to her.

"You can't tell him what we think Link was doing," Billy Jo said. "The checks, the kids… If this is as bad as I think it is, there's no way we can walk in there and tell that detective without his captain suddenly making a call and getting this shut down, leaving us nowhere."

Mark stood and reached for his jean jacket on the coat tree in the corner of his office. He shrugged it on. "Give me some credit, Billy Jo. I know what I'm doing. I'm going to give him only what I need to in order to gain access to Link's financial records. Call Gail and get her to take Harley and Lucky."

She just stared at him, then reached for her bag on the chair. "So we're really going to San Antonio?"

He gave his head a subtle shake. "We are—unless you want to stay behind."

For a moment, she thought he was serious. "Nope, I'm coming. In case you've forgotten, this is my case, and I'm the one who picked up the wrong file. I'm the one who found the check, and I'm the one now locked out of my office because it seems no one wants us digging into what Link was doing. So you know what,

Mark? I want this blown right open, and I want everyone who knows about it held accountable. And then I want to know where those kids are, each one Link had checks issued for. I want someone to answer for this."

He was standing beside her now, looking down to her. He lifted his hand to her chin and then brushed it down over her arm. "Well, let's go and get packed," he said, then strode out of the office. "Lacy, book me two seats on the float plane off the island to Seattle, then two on a flight down to San Antonio."

Billy Jo was right behind him, and Lucky was walking over to them.

"How soon do you want to leave?" Lacy said, the phone already to her ear.

"As soon as we can. Book a flight today," he said. "And, Elisha, find that girl, Kristi Moore, and when you do, call me and tell me where she is—and get me her number."

Then Mark was walking to the door, pulling it open, and gesturing for her to go through after Lucky. He reached for her arm as he closed the door. "Listen. Call Gail, but don't tell her anything, just that we're taking a few days. I don't know what we're going to find, but I have a feeling that when word starts to get out, this could quickly be shut down."

He leaned in and pressed a kiss to her lips, then strode down to his Jeep and opened the door to let Lucky jump in. "You coming?" he called out.

She made herself walk over to her car, lifting her hand. "Yeah, I'll see you at home," she said.

As she climbed behind the wheel, she thought of the call she'd made to her dad, the list of names she'd walked out with, and the places those kids were in. For a man to kill himself over a check or two, or even more, it didn't make any sense, and now she had more questions than answers.

"Damn you, Pam and Grant," she muttered. "What the hell have you done?"

Chapter 10

Billy Jo stared at concrete steps leading up to an impressive home with a manicured lawn, a big circular driveway, and a dozen or more cars, at least. The burgundy car Mark had rented at the airport, meanwhile, was parked on the road behind a pickup with a Confederate sticker on the back bumper.

"So what are we going to say when we go in there?" she said. "You said the detective is meeting us here?"

Mark wore his usual jean jacket and cowboy boots, while she was in a pair of black capris, sandals, and a sleeveless blue and green shirt she'd quickly changed into after Gail had arrived to pick up her cat and Lucky. She knew Gail was thinking this was a last-minute romantic trip away, and she had let her.

"I left him a message, so he could be here already," Mark said. "We'll just go in and see what I can see. You left a message for your dad and still haven't heard back?"

The house was filled with people, and Billy Jo watched as someone walked out, lifting a hand in a wave. Apparently, the condolence calls had started.

"He's not answering, but while you were getting the car, I talked to my mom. She said he was meeting with someone he used to work with, some senator he helped out of a jam. He didn't tell her who. I'm thinking he's finding out more about the list of institutions I sent him. I also sent him the names of the kids, and I'm glad I did, because I can't get into the CPS system anymore. Three guesses, but I would say Grant kicked me out. My password doesn't work, so…"

Mark didn't pull off his shades in the bright Texas sun. She knew he was wrapping his head around all of this. He had done some of his own research, too, after her Google searches came up with nothing.

"You know, I wish I had thought to find out whether those kids have families, mothers or fathers or whomever they were pulled from, so I could call and talk to them." She let out a sigh.

Mark nodded. "Well, if you were locked out, maybe your dad can get you something more. I hate to say it, but if you think about it, predators often get jobs working with kids—teachers, social workers, coaches…"

This was what worried her, the knowledge that those kids wouldn't be believed. "It's why I do this, because who else is going to help those kids?"

He pressed a hand to her cheek. "I know why you do what you do. I know what keeps you awake at night, and I know you see yourself in too many of those kids. You can't save them all, Billy Jo. You can do only what you can do. But here, with Link Stone, I want to take a look at the financials, too. With the suicide, they would've been able to pull everything. I'm hoping they have. Makes it easier, and then I don't have to worry about convincing Cole Mitchell to get a warrant. Seems there are a lot of people here to talk to now, not just Link's wife. This could be a good thing…"

"Are you Chief Friessen?"

Billy Jo turned to see a tall slender man with a light mustache, wearing blue jeans, a white dress shirt, cowboy boots, and a cowboy hat, walking their way.

"Mark Friessen, Roche Harbor Police. Are you Detective Murphy?"

"That would be me," he said with a slight twang. "I see you found it okay. Sorry I didn't answer the phone when you called. Has been a little crazy today." He had a wide stride, and he met them quickly and held his hand out to Mark. "Ma'am," he then said, inclining his head toward her.

"This is Billy Jo McCabe. She's helping out on the case. Have you spoken with Mrs. Stone since I called you?" Mark said.

The detective gestured to the house. "I called and spoke with one of the daughters, asked if we could come by, as we had some questions. Seems they have a lot of friends and family. I am curious, though. I pulled the financials, and Link Stone had a substantial amount of money in his account, almost sixty-eight million. You say he was a social worker? Didn't know they made that kind of money."

Billy Jo wondered whether she'd heard right. "Sixty-eight million, you sure about that?"

The detective gestured to the front door, and Billy Jo fell in beside Mark as they started up the side steps. "Checked it twice," he said. "A lot of deposits, but I only went back a year. Have my partner putting in a request for the last five, but I wonder how far back I should go. So you want to fill me in on what we're looking at here? You said he's a social worker for vulnerable kids."

Billy Jo's chest tightened as the detective reached for the bell and pressed it. The chime echoed outside.

"I'm not sure what's going on, exactly," Mark said, "other than that checks payable to kids were signed over to Mr. Stone, and from what I've been able to put together, he cashed them."

The detective looked right at Mark with his brown eyes, unsmiling, then glanced at Billy Jo. "You talked to the kids?"

Billy Jo's heart thudded, and Mark pulled off his sunglasses, glancing down to her and then back to the detective. "That's the thing," she said. "I couldn't find the kids. They were placed with institutions, but for the two I called, the numbers were disconnected."

The detective was looking right at her, shaking his head, and his expression left her with a sick feeling in her stomach. Mark said nothing.

"You evidently have some idea, Detective?" Billy Jo said.

Then the door opened to reveal a young woman with dark hair, her eyes red rimmed as if she'd been crying, with voices in the background.

"I'm Detective Murphy, and these are Chief Friessen and Billy Jo, from Roche Harbor. I'm wondering if we can talk with Mrs. Stone."

The young woman pressed a Kleenex to her cheek to wipe away a tear. "Yes, of course. Come in, please. I spoke with you on the phone. I'm Lynn. My mom, Melinda, is in the kitchen."

Mark gestured for Billy Jo to go first, and she stepped inside, looking up at the impressive staircase, the high ceiling, and the entryway. This home was stunning.

She heard voices off to the side from a big living room, and the door closed behind her. Mark and the detective stood there as Lynn gestured down a wide hall.

"Down this way. I'll take you in," she said, then started walking.

Mark fell in behind her, but the detective reached out and stopped Billy Jo before she could follow.

"You mentioned checks," he said, his voice low, "but what I saw were large deposits. Unless your checks were for hundreds of thousands, then I think you and I both know that this wasn't just him taking checks."

She stared at the detective and wondered if the

sound she heard was her ears ringing. "I think you'd better say what you think it is, then," she said.

Ahead, Mark was walking down the hall, following Lynn. Billy Jo took in the impressive house and fell in beside Detective Murphy.

"You want me to spell it out?" he said. "Then I will. Trafficking kids is big business."

Yeah, that was exactly what she hadn't wanted this to be.

Chapter 11

"That's my mom over there," Lynn told Mark as he followed her into the kitchen.

Melinda Stone was a petite woman with short dark hair, setting cookies on a plate. Two other women stood with her, one on the chunky side, washing dishes, another making coffee. A slender older man was also there, leaning against the fridge. The energy in the room was one of death, despair, and grief.

Mark tucked his sunglasses in his shirtfront as he followed Lynn over to Melinda, who picked up the plate and spilled the cookies on the floor.

"Oh no!" she cried out.

"Mom, it's okay. I'll get it." Lynn quickly leaned down to pick up the plate, and the other women helped Melinda up. Mark glanced around. Their faces were solemn, family and friends, he thought, just being there to support a loved one.

"Mom, this is Chief Friessen, from Roche Harbor."

She lifted her gaze, and he felt horrible.

"I am so sorry for your loss, Mrs. Stone. I know this is not a great time. I'm wondering if I could talk to you and ask you a few questions."

She looked past him, and he glanced back to where the detective was standing with Billy Jo. From the expression on her face, he knew something was bothering her, and he inclined his head.

"Melinda, sorry to intrude," Detective Murphy said. "We won't stay long, but we really wanted to talk with you about Link, just a few questions…"

"Really, Detective, you think this is the time?" said the heavyset woman with deep brown hair, thick and short. Mark didn't know who she was. "He just killed himself. Can't you leave the family in peace?"

"It's fine, Rita," Melinda said. "I just don't know what else I can tell you. Or do you have any idea why he killed himself?"

Mark moved off to the side, and somehow Detective Murphy had Link's wife walking out of the kitchen and into a sunroom, where she opened the double doors to lead them out to an impressive backyard, with a huge pool and patio, the kind that screamed money. He followed Billy Jo out.

"You okay?" he said to her as she slid her hand on his arm.

"I'm looking at this house, this place, and what I see is a man who did something big. The detective told me something. With the money here, and sixty-eight million in his accounts, you know what we're talking about, right?"

He stared down at Billy Jo. Damn, he could read her so well. Then he glanced to the detective walking just ahead of them with Link's wife. "Yeah. If you can't find the kids, they were sold. Come on, are you good with this? Because I'm not. Let's talk to the wife. You'd think she'd know something."

Billy Jo nodded and let her hand fall away as they approached Melinda and Murphy, who were standing now at a big fountain. The water was soothing, but the situation was creepy.

"I told you before, Detective, I wish I understood why he did it. We were so happy. Our daughter is getting married, and now she doesn't have a father to give her away. This makes no sense."

"You said you didn't understand what he meant in the note he left, where he said he was sorry," Murphy said. Mark didn't know the detective well, but he was a guest there, and he had to remind himself of that.

"Sorry that he killed himself, is that what he meant?" Melinda said. She wore a white sleeveless blouse and navy capris, with a simple gold band on her ring finger. "I don't know… We were so happy. He was retired. We were traveling, really enjoying life. I don't understand. Was he in trouble?"

"Your husband was a social worker, is that right?" Murphy said. "His last job was in Roche Harbor?"

Melinda pulled her arms over her chest. "Yes and no. He was offered another job in Wyoming, and he went out there first while I packed up the house on the island and sold it. Then he called and said we were moving to San Antonio. Not sure what happened, but he said he was getting out of the business. He couldn't take pulling one more kid from a bad situation. It was hard on my husband. He cared a lot for those kids…"

"This is the house he bought, on a social worker's salary?" Mark cut in.

She stilled. "Are you implying something, Chief? I'll have you know my husband received an inheritance from an aunt, which is one of the reasons he retired and didn't take the job in Wyoming. I hope you're not implying he did something?" She jabbed her finger toward her chest.

"No, ma'am, we're not implying anything like that, but we suspect maybe someone had something on your husband," the detective said. He had a smooth way of talking. He flicked his brown eyes to Mark and then back to the widow. "I'm wondering if your husband kept any papers or an office or something that we could take a look at to get an idea of what happened. It could be that someone was coming at him with blackmail, lies, anything, and maybe he didn't think he had any other option. I can tell you, ma'am, there are some sick people out there. I've seen it. They know how to spin something and put enough pressure on someone that he suddenly snaps."

Melinda Stone had an odd expression of grief and confusion, and Mark wondered if she'd say no. Damn, the detective was good. Then she nodded. "He had an office upstairs, but I'm wondering if I should call our lawyer and you should go through it with him. Maybe that would be better…"

"Ah, Mrs. Stone, we could do that, but it would take some time, and I'm just hoping to close this up so we can be on our way. Do you think your husband wouldn't want you to know if someone was trying to hurt him or you?"

She seemed to consider, then lifted her hands. "Well, okay, I guess it couldn't hurt to let you have a look. Come on." She gestured and started walking, and the detective tossed him an easy look.

Billy Jo reached for his arm again as they were walking and said in a low voice, "I don't feel good about this, Mark."

"You want to find out what he was doing?" he said. He wondered if her issue was a moral one because her dad was a lawyer, but she said nothing else as they followed Melinda into the house past other people, men and women, all dressed well and all looking their way.

Melinda had led them up the massive stairwell to the second floor when her daughter called out, "Mom, what are you doing?"

Melinda gestured to a room in the middle of the hall and opened the double doors. "In here is his office," she said to the detective, then leaned over the railing, looking down. "They're just taking a look at your dad's office."

Mark didn't hear what Lynn said in reply as he walked into a room with big windows, a dark wood bookshelf on one wall, a massive mahogany desk with a phone, and a fireplace with a framed family photo hanging above it.

"If you'll excuse me, I'll just ask that you don't make a mess and put everything back as it is," Melinda said.

Billy Jo was staring at the books, while Mark took in the detective, who was standing at the window, looking out.

"We won't be long," Murphy drawled. "Thank you again, Mrs. Stone."

Mark watched as she walked away, leaving them in an office that belonged to a man he was more than convinced had had his hand in something.

"You realize that if we find anything without a warrant, it's inadmissible," Mark said. Behind him, Billy Jo had pulled out a book and was flipping through it. Then she shoved it back on the shelf.

"We're just looking, remember?" said the detective. He reached down to pull open the big bottom drawer of the desk, but it was locked, so Mark walked around and pulled on the top side drawer, but it was also locked.

The detective pulled open the middle drawer and shot him a look as he held up a set of keys from within. He sat down in the big leather chair, trying one key and then another from the three on the ring. Billy Jo was still looking through the bookshelf.

"Ah, here we are," the detective said as he pulled open the drawer. It was neatly organized, filled with stuffed folders labeled "house," "internet," "phone," and "gas." The detective rummaged through them, and Mark lifted his gaze again to stare at the large photo above the fireplace across the room, unable to figure out what was off.

"I don't know what I'm looking for, but it appears to be just household stuff, far better organized than I've ever been," Murphy said.

Mark walked over to fireplace, to the photo in a deep brown frame of Melinda smiling with Lynn, the other daughter, and Link Stone. He reached for the end of it, and it swung out from the wall, where there was a safe.

"Hey, look at this." Mark gestured over his shoulder, where Billy Jo was holding another book.

The detective stood up from the chair and closed the drawer. "A safe. You think we can get the missus to open that for us?"

"No one is opening anything," cut in someone from the doorway. "I'm Bill Roberts, the family lawyer. You have a warrant here, Detective?" He wore a navy suit and glasses, with dark hair, and he strode in, headed right for him. Melinda and Lynn were there, looking at him, and no one looked happy.

"No, do we need a warrant?" Detective Murphy said. "We asked Mrs. Stone if we could look around, and she was fine with it. We're just trying to understand why Link Stone hanged himself. This is an investigation."

"Let me see. You said he hanged himself, so there is no foul play," Roberts said. "He left a note. This family has been through enough. You're not searching through anything in this office or house without a warrant. I'm going to ask you to leave—now."

He was very direct. Mark knew when a lawyer couldn't be pushed.

"Sure, let's go," said Billy Jo, already wrapping her sweater around herself, her arms crossed, and she tilted her head toward the door. Meanwhile, Melinda and Lynn were glaring at them as if they'd seen something they shouldn't have.

Mark followed Billy Jo out, the detective behind him. He didn't meet the eyes of anyone watching them leave. The front door was opened for them, and all he could think of was that whatever was in that safe, he wanted to know.

"Well, that sucked," the detective drawled as they strode down the concrete steps. "Seems someone called the family pit bull. What do you think he knows something, from the way he went off?"

"I'm sure he did, but I found something in one of the books, a list of names and amounts," Billy Jo said. She unfolded a piece of paper and held it out to Mark, who settled his hand on her lower back as they kept walking. The detective was right there with them as they walked off the property toward the rental car parked on the side of the road.

"Look at the first name on the list," Billy Jo said, pointing at it. "Don't you see? This all started with Deena Rae."

Chapter 12

The San Antonio police department was big, with staff hurrying through the hallways, phones ringing. The homicide department had seven desks with partitions, with two chairs in front of the old desk that belonged to Detective Murphy.

"You think we can trust him?" Billy Jo said as she scanned her phone, legs crossed, her foot touching Mark's leg as he sprawled out in the chair beside her and turned toward her.

He made a face and shook his head. "Not sure, maybe. He hasn't given me any reason to doubt him…"

"Okay, good news," Detective Murphy said, reappearing before them. "My captain is just talking to the DA now and getting a warrant for that safe. Would've given anything to talk to the widow, though, and she'd likely have opened it. The lawyer showing up was bad timing, that's for sure."

The detective was still wearing his cream-colored cowboy hat as he leaned down on his desk. Billy Jo had to remind herself that what she was feeling was just her lack of trust in authority, which she figured would always be there.

"So where's the paper with the list of names?" she said, hearing how sharply it had come out.

The detective sat down in a rather nice high-end black chair. The way he raised his brows and offered her a mocking smile, she wondered if that was the reason for the dislike she suddenly felt. Maybe it was because she was a woman or something. Mark was staring right at her.

"You worried about something?" Murphy said. Now it sounded as if he were playing a game.

"Detective Murphy, quit jerking us around," Mark cut in. "Billy Jo asked you a question. Do not disrespect her. You took the list of names she found and walked off to your captain, and now here we are, waiting for a warrant. Although I have no authority—"

"That's right, Chief. You're a guest here," the detective drawled. Then he dragged his gaze over to Billy Jo, and she didn't know what to make of the way he was watching her. "Meant no disrespect. The captain has the list. Whereabouts did you find it again?"

In a book about eroding soil, she remembered, but she wasn't going to tell him that. The books had been about the most boring, meaningless subjects. Her hunch had paid off.

"Just one of the books, tucked in there, hidden. I mean, who would think to look inside all those books?"

He didn't pull his gaze, and she didn't know what to make of that, because gone was the detective who had been on their side. She shrugged and glanced over to Mark, and she knew his expression well. He'd figured out that something wasn't quite right.

"You were the one who had the idea to get into the office and search it, Detective," Mark said. "We have a list of names, and one of them is a girl, Deena Rae. This all started with a check signed over to Link Stone. You're the one who brought up the sixty-eight million in his account. Isn't that what you said?"

The detective was staring at them, then leaned forward and looked past him. Billy Jo turned to see who she thought was the captain walking their way—dark hair, average height, a brown dress shirt and tie.

"Okay, the warrant is signed," the captain said. "You can head over. It's for the safe only. The tech will meet you there."

Mark was standing, and he had several inches on the man, who held his hand out.

"Captain Diego. You must be the Roche Harbour police chief."

"That's right, Mark Friessen, and this is Billy Jo McCabe, the social worker who discovered something was off about Link Stone. Several checks were signed over to him by kids for whom he was the social worker of record, and he then cashed them."

The captain held his hand out to her, and his

handshake was brief, hard, his eyes dark. He nodded to the side. "Let's take this into my office."

Mark slid his hand over Billy Jo's back as she stepped in front of him, following the captain into an office around the corner. The detective closed the door behind them.

"Sorry for all this cloak and dagger," the captain said, moving around his desk, where Billy Jo spotted the list of names and amounts. So there it was. She wanted to pull out her cell phone and take a photo of it, which she would have done earlier if the detective hadn't taken it. "This list of names, you found it?" Captain Diego gestured to her.

"That's right," she said, adding nothing more.

The captain lifted his gaze to the detective, and something passed between them, and she had an awful feeling.

"What's going on here?" Mark said. "Why am I getting the feeling you're holding something back?" He turned to the detective, who was leaning against the door.

"You have any idea what this is?" The captain lifted the paper and held it out, and the knot in Billy Jo's stomach left her with a sick feeling now.

Mark said nothing, then dragged his gaze to her. "I think you'd better tell us, Captain."

"Those numbers beside the names aren't payment amounts." It was the detective who spoke instead, pushing away from the door. "They're locations. And I'm sorry if I sounded off before, but we had to be sure you weren't involved."

Billy Jo wasn't sure she'd heard him right.

"What the hell are you talking about? Involved in what?" Mark said. He had a way about him when he was frustrated, and she didn't need to say anything, just watched their reactions. She could see now that they knew something, and she wondered whether they'd share it.

"We've been investigating a black market ring for a few years. It operates from a few parts of the country, Minnesota, Colorado, California, and one of the Pacific Northwest islands. When you called about Link Stone and we looked into his financials, he'd never been on our radar. These names on this list, you said you found them in a book? We're going to need to know where and which one, because these names are of kids who have disappeared and been sold. We suspect this ring of dealing in everything, from selling babies, to human trafficking, to organ harvesting."

Billy Jo knew her mouth had to be gaping. "Organs, as in…"

"Yeah, as bad as you think," Detective Murphy said. "Organs for transplant, bought on the black market, anything and everything, kidneys, lungs, hearts… Sick shit like that happens. Ten of the names on this list match bodies that washed up with organs missing. They were kids, teenagers, ages eight to twelve. You have no idea the market for healthy organs from kids. This investigation has been off the books, as we didn't know who was involved, but we know there is someone running this, and it's not Link Stone. There are likely a few players who are disposable, but this ring isn't small, and I guarantee you it's international."

"Wait, are you saying Link Stone was selling kids?" Billy Jo lifted her hand. She thought her ears were ringing.

There was a knock at the door then, and the detective opened it. Someone handed him a file, and he closed the door and walked back over to the captain's desk to open it. She wanted to yell. This couldn't be happening. Mark's face said everything she was feeling.

"CPS is one of the best places to grab kids," the captain said, "especially when no one is looking for them. I'd suggest this may be bigger than we believe. How many kids did he pull from homes? And of those, how many can you account for, and over how long, how many years? Then there's the bigger question of who else is involved. I'd say once we can answer those questions, we may be able to at least put a dent in some part of this."

Billy Jo stared at the captain, who was now sitting in his chair behind the desk. "What about finding the kids?"

He shot her a cold and unfeeling look. "Finding the kids? That would be ideal but not realistic. These kids are gone, Ms. McCabe, sold, dead—or, for some of the girls, trafficked and living a nightmare. It's sick, isn't it? So get over to the Stone house. If Mrs. Stone won't open the safe, then get a torch to it and break it open. Go through that entire office and find anything and everything," the captain said to Detective

Murphy, then dragged his gaze over to Mark. "And just remember, Chief, you're a guest here. You can be there, but stay out of the way."

The detective was already at the door, pulling it open, and he stepped out.

The captain was now looking at her. "Ms. McCabe, I'm not unfeeling, but I already know the outcome of this case, and it isn't a happy one. No one will blame you if you get on a plane and go home."

She felt Mark's hand reaching for hers, taking it, that solid strength that pulled her along. She stepped beside him, and he said to the captain, all the while looking at her, "Billy Jo is fine, and neither one of us is getting on a plane until we have answers."

Damn, he was too perfect and knew her too well. As Mark led her out of the office, following the detective, she didn't once let go of his hand.

Chapter 13

Cops were everywhere in the house, and Mark knew both of Link Stone's daughters and his widow, Melinda, were being questioned by another detective. A welder was burning through the metal of the safe, and four other cops in the office had pulled out every book from the bookshelf and dumped them in a pile on the floor. The desk had been emptied, and a hidden door in the bookshelf had been opened.

Detective Murphy had gone inside, where there were shelves of papers and books. One was an album of photos of kids, which he had brought to the desk, and Billy Jo was going through it now. Instead of names, each child had only a number.

"You want to take a break, grab a coffee or something?" Mark asked her.

She shook her head and kept flipping the pages. "The detective said there are twenty-five other albums, and these photos are dated going back years,

Mark. I'd say these here are fifteen years old, at least. They each have a number, no name. I guess it's easier to catalog them that way, kind of like livestock: age, sex, breed… This is despicable, and this monster is the one CPS is protecting. You think Grant knows? You think CPS now knows and they're doing damage control? Is that why I was walked out of the office? How many senior officials do you think are involved? Someone in accounting, maybe? Worse, I've called my dad and left several messages, and I haven't heard back from him. He was looking into those companies, those institutions. How much do you want to bet that they don't exist?"

She was now looking up at him, understanding the gravity of what they were seeing. She was so damn strong, whereas he didn't think he'd be able to shut his eyes that night without imagining the horror of what had happened to those kids.

"It's open," one of the cops called out.

Mark had to fight his first instinct to walk over to the safe. Detective Murphy was there already, pulling out a flash drive, a small black accounting book, and what looked like stacks of cash.

"There's gold too," he said to one of the cops. "Bag up everything, including this. Get it to forensics. They'll have to go through all of it." Then he was walking over to Mark, and he let out a heavy sigh, flipping through the black book, shaking his head. "This is just numbers. Could be locations, a code, I don't know. I'll have to have our computer techs, forensics, the entire team go through this. I know this is not the answer you wanted, but I think this is the end of the line, Chief. It's going to take the team a while to sort through this. The widow is being taken in, and she'll be questioned. Same with the daughters. They say they don't know anything…"

Mark's cell phone buzzed, and he pulled it from inside his jean jacket and saw a private caller, knowing it was likely his office. "I have to take this," he said, then turned away and answered the phone. "Mark Friessen."

The detective was talking to Billy Jo as Mark stepped out of the room, where it was quieter.

"Chief, it's Elisha. Sorry it took me so long, but I tracked down Kristi Moore."

He shook his head, because it was kind of a moot point now. "Thanks, Elisha, but I've got my hands full right now, and this case has turned into something else, the kind of trafficking ring I never expected. Let Ms. Moore know I'll call her when I get back. Billy Jo and I should be flying back tomorrow…"

"Chief, I think you're going to want to talk to her now, because I just got off the phone with her, and she told me a bizarre story. She said Link Stone told her he was setting up an account for her and was having the state send her money, because he could, for anything—school supplies, medical care, clothes, extracurricular activities. He took her checks, and when she was sixteen and needed money, she called him about the account. He told her he would meet her to discuss it. She said when she showed up at the address he'd given her, a small cafe at the edge of town, she had a bad feeling. When she walked in, there was no one inside but another man, sitting there, watching her.

"Link Stone locked the door after her, and she knew this wasn't anything good. She said he asked her to sit, and she said no, she just wanted her money, every one of those checks he made her sign over and said he would keep for her because she didn't have a bank account. She said she had a friend waiting outside for her, and she pointed to the window and told Link it was her boyfriend in the car out front, and his mother and father also knew she was there. She said she didn't know why, but she just had a feeling something bad was going to happen.

"She said he became angry and told her she had nothing coming, and he grabbed her, so she screamed and bit him and then ran out the door. She went to the sheriff, but she said she knew she wouldn't be believed. The sheriff brushed it off because she had been labeled difficult, a compulsive liar, and her credibility had been shredded. From what you've just said, Chief, it sounds like her having the foresight to bring someone with her may have saved her. Just so you know, she's now married, has two kids, and has put herself through night school. She teaches grade two."

Mark glanced back to the door, seeing Billy Jo close up the book. The detective had been handed a box of evidence. Mark nodded and said, "Send me her number. I'll call her." Then he hung up.

Billy Jo was walking his way, and all he could wonder was how many more children like Kristi were out there. He figured what Kristi may not have known was that her photo could very well have ended up in one of those albums. He felt a cold terror, realizing what a man who had been working in his community, on his island, had done right under the noses of everyone who lived there.

"Who was that?" Billy Jo said. "The detective said they're wrapping up here. Nothing more we can do."

He nodded, his heart thumping, feeling that cold, sick feeling, and looked over her head to the office of Link Stone. Would they ever understand the depths of his depravity? Sick, sociopathic, yet he'd appeared to be just the average family guy.

"Mark?" Billy Jo said again. She ran her hand over his arm and then down, reaching for his hand, and he didn't let go.

"That was Elisha. She tracked down Kristi Moore," he said. Billy Jo looked up at him and nodded, and he continued. "I'll give her a call and talk to her, but I have a feeling she doesn't know how lucky she is. She could have ended up like the kids in those books, just a number, never to be seen again."

Billy Jo stepped closer and slid her hands around his waist, hugging him. This was the first time he'd ever felt her trembling. He wrapped his arms around her and held her.

"Hey, it's going to be okay," he said, but she shook her head against him and looked up to him, pressing her chin against his chest.

"No, Mark, it's not. The detective said his captain has already put a call in to CPS in every state. They said it's going to take some time to find out who these kids are, and he told me the reality is that with some, they'll never know. How many are from the island? You think Grant will still stonewall me and cover this up?"

She stepped back, and Mark slid his hands over her shoulders, watching boxes being carried out behind her by cops, down the stairs to the open front door.

"I figure Grant will throw you under the bus, or Pam, or someone else. Whatever it is, he'll save his own skin."

Her brow furrowed, and he sensed the anger she was entitled to feel as she let out a rude sound.

"But if he tries to use you as a scapegoat," he continued, "no one will find his body when I'm through with him."

He wasn't sure if that was a smile or a wince.

She flicked her blue eyes up to him. "You'd kill him for me, huh?"

Yup, it was a smile.

"Someone who tries to hurt you? Without blinking an eye."

She wrapped her arms around his shoulders and rose up on her tiptoes, and he pulled her closer again and pressed a kiss to her lips. Then he stepped back, wrapped his arm around her shoulder, pulling her close, and said, "Let's go home."

Chapter 14

As the float plane landed and docked, the sun had already gone down. Billy Jo was sitting in the passenger seat beside the pilot, wearing a headset. Mark had given the seat up to her, hoping it would make her feel better, and sitting in back gave him a minute to wrap his head around this nightmare. How many kids from the island had disappeared? He stared at the text on his phone from the detective in San Antonio. It was worse than he'd thought, and he didn't want to tell Billy Jo anymore.

Was this what his dad had meant when he said that sometimes a man had to carry the weight of something alone to protect his family?

The pilot was now shutting off the noisy float plane and stepping out his side door. Billy Jo glanced back to him in the dark and lifted off her headset, then unfastened her seatbelt. Mark opened his door and stepped out onto the dock, then reached for Billy Jo. The pilot pulled out their overnight bag, which they hadn't ended up using, and Mark reached for it, then took Billy Jo's hand and started up the dock.

"Should we swing by to pick up Lucky and Harley?" she said.

He knew it was late, and Gail and the chief were the kind of people who went to bed early. It was past nine, as the lights on the dock shone bright, illuminating his Jeep, parked in the lot off to the side.

"In the morning," he said. "Let's just go home, get some sleep."

She didn't reply. They walked in silence, and he pulled his hand free to unlock the Jeep and open the back to toss in the suitcase. Billy Jo was already in the passenger side, sitting quietly as he slid behind the wheel and started the engine. He flicked on the lights and pulled out.

"You think I still have a job?" she said.

He hadn't expected that, and he looked over to her in the dark, wondering where it had come from. "Of course you do—unless you don't want your job? I wouldn't blame you after all this."

She let out a heavy sigh. He made his way out of downtown and geared down on the road that led to his cabin.

"You know, Mark, after learning what Link did, there's no way I could sleep at night if I walked out, knowing another Link could take my place. How many kids disappeared?"

He didn't look over to her. The edge to her voice had him squeezing the steering wheel harder than necessary.

"Tomorrow, I'll walk in there," she continued, "Grant be damned, and pull every one of Link's files to see how many kids I can track down, make sure they're okay—or as okay as they can be. If he was selling kids, why take the checks too? How much do you think he took from CPS, from the kids who were supposed to get the money?"

Damn, she had a lot of questions, and he'd have given anything to have the answers. As he pulled down the narrow road, he spotted light spilling from his cabin.

"Did we leave a light on?" he said as he pulled in, but he quickly spotted Billy Jo's car and realized it was Chase McCabe sitting outside under the porch light. Lucky's tail was wagging as he ran across the deck.

Mark parked and turned off the Jeep. "Your dad's here," was all he said, then opened his door. The interior light popped on, and Billy Jo shot him a puzzled expression. He knew she hadn't been able to get a hold of Chase, yet there he stood, with his light hair, a dark pullover sweater, blue jeans, and a smile for Billy Jo when she stepped out of the Jeep. Lucky went to her first.

"Dad, what are you doing here? And how did you get in?" she said, running her hand over Lucky, who then trotted over to Mark, and her gaze followed him.

"Come on over here and give me a hug first," Chase said. "Missed you. I got your message but wanted to talk in person. I called and talked with your new deputy, Elisha, and she said Gail and Tolly Shephard had your dog and cat and weren't expecting you back until tomorrow. Gail has a key, and she let me in after she picked me up at the dock. Took a float plane in. Was just as easy for me to take the dog and cat tonight."

Chase hugged Billy Jo until it was too much for her, and he let her go. Then he held his hand out and said, "Good to see you, Mark."

"You, too."

Chase gave his hand a heavy squeeze and then patted his shoulder.

"So you just flew here? This is kind of odd," Mark said. He figured he'd say it even if Billy Jo wouldn't, as Chase had just made himself at home. Maybe he needed to dial it back a bit, though. This was Billy Jo's father.

Something about Chase's expression changed, reflecting the reality of what he'd uncovered, and that made it all too real. "I wanted to talk with both of you, and it's the kind of conversation I didn't want to have over the phone."

Mark gestured to the door, but Chase only shook his head and said, "No, let's keep this outside. I checked into the names of those companies and institutions for you, but the call I made got me nowhere. I was told they didn't exist. You sent me names of missing kids, ones in institutions that exist only on paper. I found out enough. These kids didn't have anyone. No one was looking for them. I realized from the second call I made that there was something nefarious going on. I know someone in Washington who can access anything, the kind of person who can help fix a problem, but even he told me that whatever this is, it was bigger than him. Someone would've been given a heads-up the moment I made the call."

Mark knew Billy Jo understood exactly what her dad was saying. "So is that why Link Stone hanged himself?" She turned to Mark. He wondered if Chase already knew.

"We just flew back from San Antonio," he explained, "where Stone had retired with sixty-eight million in his account. He hanged himself in his garage and left a note that said he was sorry."

Chase nodded, his arms crossed, and glanced back to the house. "Hey, sweetheart, you should go and check on your cat. Gail said something about him not eating. I'm sure he's fine. Could be he just needs to see you."

Billy Jo hesitated only a second before worry for her cat hit her and she started for the door. Chase just stood there, his arms still crossed, looking out, and Mark realized he had something to say to him.

"You know, Mark, I love my daughter, and I don't want her hurt. Some of the things this social worker did leave me feeling an icy chill I've never felt before."

Mark stared, realizing Billy Jo's dad knew her so well. He could see her through the window now, holding her cat, instead of out there, where he'd expected her to be.

"How bad is it?" he said. "There were lots of photos of kids, with numbers and records I have no idea how to make sense of. The San Antonio PD are investigating, but I know Billy Jo wants to go through every one of Link Stone's files and find out which kids are accounted for and which are missing."

Chase had lines around his eyes. Mark realized his girl's father likely knew things he would never know. "Mark, a child goes missing every forty seconds in this country, and the motivation is often money—from sex trafficking, to rogue FBI and CIA operations, to the selling of babies. I've found links to the Ukrainian embassy, and there's a county in Minnesota that goes through the church to draft a legal record, a birth certificate, saying a girl had her baby while there, when in fact the document creates a new record for a child that's been taken, and then they get it out of the county. Or a doctor's note will say the child is disabled and has to be moved to such and such a place because the parents have inadequate conditions to regulate the child.

"It's all about getting the right people to fill out the right paperwork. Brokering kids is big business, and it goes deeper than a social worker who was paid a few million. This is a trillion-dollar industry, reaching into a shadow government that no one knows or sees. This has been going on for decades. My daughter picked up a file no one was supposed to see. You have any idea how many children disappear within Child Protective Services every year?"

Mark didn't want to answer. He realized Chase knew something he didn't want his daughter to know. "A lot, I take it. Why?"

Chase shook his head. "It's an elaborate scheme. The unwanted, no one will miss them or be looking."

Mark had to make himself swallow the heavy lump.

Inside, Billy Jo was at the sink, filling a bowl with water. Then Lucky was pawing at the door, and she opened it and let him in. "Are you two coming in?" she called out.

"Yeah, just letting your dad grill me and make sure I'm looking after you," Mark replied.

She only rolled her eyes, then shook her head before closing the door. He wasn't sure if her dad was amused as he stared out into the darkness.

"I'd rather she not know everything," Chase said. "You know there's a black market for organs, especially from children and babies, and you know kids are being sold to pedophiles. It's fucking sick that a social worker was here for how long and likely did this everywhere else he worked, in each town, and no one knew. No one questioned. Because no one wants to believe something like this could happen right under their watch. I suspect the San Antonio police will arrest a few front men who'll be sacrificed, but they'll never catch the ones running it. It's too big. The kids are held in New York, California, Washington, maybe, and that's just me guessing. They'll be moved, likely underground, via private planes and islands. They'll be five steps ahead because of people on the inside, like the social worker who picked off these children." Chase was looking right at him.

Mark nodded. "The detective texted me and said they raided an underground bunker. It was massive, with tunnels and cages. They found forty kids, but two didn't make it. They also learned about a wine tour organization in the Napa Valley that would target women, taking the ones who had no one looking out for them. The detective didn't think I would want Billy Jo to know, either, and I don't, because I know it'll be something else that haunts her. I don't want it in my own head, but I'll keep it so she doesn't have to."

Chase reached over and slapped his arm. "You're a good man, Mark. So Billy Jo told me you're looking at real estate."

So that was it. He shrugged, wondering how Chase could just shrug it off, because Mark was still shaken. "Yeah, a bigger place, you know…"

There it was—a smile, he thought. "You're taking your time. Get a house first and then what, ease her in gradually? I expect you'll talk to me first."

Mark hadn't considered going to Chase, because this was Billy Jo. "I can't rush her. Baby steps, but when I ask her…"

Chase reached over again and squeezed his shoulder. "When you ask my daughter to marry you, you do it right." Then he had him turned and walking back to the house. "Oh, and the Carmen thing? Consider her off the no-fly list."

Mark realized this man had the kind of reach most people didn't. "So who did you call, a senator, a congressman, someone in Washington?"

Chase reached for the doorknob and turned it, then pushed open the door. "Someone who owes me," he said.

Chapter 15

Her dad had slept on the sofa, and when Billy Jo left for the office, he was just getting up. Mark, meanwhile, was already gone after having spoken for an hour on the phone with Kristi Moore, from Minnesota.

Now Billy Jo had a dragon to slay—namely Grant, who had taken her key and her files. She wasn't going to let him separate the Gillespie girls. She was furious because kids didn't have a voice, and she realized she would do anything to make sure nothing happened to the ones on her watch.

She pulled up in front of the office and spotted a beige SUV along with Pam's red Fiat. She stepped out of her car, pulled in a breath, pushed her shoulders back, and strode to the door. She pulled on it once, but it was locked, so she fisted her hand and knocked, and she didn't have to wait long before spotting Pam on the other side.

She heard the deadbolt and pulled the door open

to step inside, and Pam stepped back, and for a moment she wasn't sure whether she'd tell her to leave, that she wasn't supposed to be there or something.

"Did Grant know you were coming?" Pam said. She didn't move, so Billy Jo walked around her.

"Nope. So where is he, my office?" She knew Pam was right behind her, and ahead was Grant, walking out of her office, holding a file.

"Pam, listen. I need you to call…" Grant started, then spotted her and closed up the file. She forced a smile to her face, but she'd rather have slugged him. "Billy Jo, what are you doing here?"

"Well, one, I work here, and I'm not going to let you run me out. You know where I was yesterday? I can see you're both dying to know, from your shocked looks. I was in San Antonio with my boyfriend—you know, the chief of police. Let's talk about Link Stone, the social worker you were such good friends with, Pam. And you, Grant, what was your relationship with him? The nice detective we met down there was handling Link's suicide, as he hanged himself in his garage. Did you know the home he bought down there was worth nearly two million dollars, and on a social worker's salary? What's more, did you know he had sixty-eight million in his bank account?"

She wasn't sure whether they already knew. She didn't think she'd ever seen Pam look so upset. Her face was pale and her eyes appeared bloodshot. Grant was still holding those files, and the way he worked his mouth, she was wondering whether he was trying to figure out what to say or not say.

"I was briefed by CPS this morning, Billy Jo," he finally said. "We are completely shocked, and we had no idea this was happening right under our noses. Link fooled a lot of people, and right now the commissioner, deputy commissioner, chief financial officer, and executives for intake are all meeting and pulling everything he had, every case he handled and consulted on, nearly two hundred thousand cases in his time with CPS in three states. Everyone is combing through every file. Now, I know things got a little heated here, and I understand your frustration. I hear you, I really do, and I understand it. We'll get it all sorted."

She just stared at him. "Sorted, really? Link Stone was a predator. He preyed on kids. He was part of a heinous underground plot to sell kids on the black market, and those he didn't sell he somehow convinced to sign their CPS checks over to him, and he was keeping the money. Will you bother to look into that too, or is CPS trying to figure out how to bury it so word doesn't get out? You know you can't have the public learning that a social worker was stealing kids, stealing their checks. It wouldn't look good." She knew she was pushing it, but she wasn't going to give them a pass.

Grant let out a heavy sigh. "Look, I'm still trying to get my head around all this. All I know is what I was told, which is that they're investigating. I have people to report to, as well. In the meantime, there are kids that have to be looked after. Billy Jo, you're right about the Gillespie girls. I had a word with the Fitzpatricks about their concerns, and it would probably be best if you spoke with them. The girls are still there. It seems their concerns are mostly financial."

She made herself pull in a breath, then waited as Grant reached into his pocket and pulled out a key to hold out to her.

"Your key," he said.

She hesitated only a second before taking it.

"I'm sorry I came down on you so hard," he said, "but let's try to move past this."

She heard pounding on the front door, then a rattle, and turned to see Mark there. She didn't wait for Grant or Pam to say anything, just strode to the door and flicked the lock, and he pulled it open, his gaze going right to her.

"Everything okay?" he said.

Damn, she really loved him. "Yeah, got my key back." She held it up, but she could see he wasn't amused, as he lifted a brow and looked past her. He pressed his hand to her arm and rubbed it, then headed over to Grant.

"You and I are going to settle some things," Mark said, pointing right at him. For a second, as she watched Mark really digging into his steps, she thought Grant's face paled. He took a step back, and he looked scared.

Mark looked back to her. "That's my girl you stepped on and treated like a piece of shit for doing a job you should have been doing," he said. "If you ever again treat her with the kind of disrespect you did, I will make your life a living hell. I will become your worst nightmare. I will take your life apart and dig up any piece of dirt I can find, and then I will make sure everyone on this island knows that your first response was to protect a predator who hunted kids, sold them, and stole from them. Your life will be worth shit, and you can file all the complaints you want about me, but I will keep coming for you." Mark actually jabbed his finger at Grant's chest, and Billy Jo was too stunned to say anything. She'd never seen this caveman side of Mark, not with her.

"Look, I already apologized to Billy Jo," Grant said. "None of us here had any idea. This has never happened before. It was a misunderstanding, is all…"

She thought Grant even stuttered. For the first time in this shitty mess, she couldn't help but smile, and she took one step and another until she was standing right beside Mark. She pressed her hand to his arm, and when he finally pulled his gaze from Grant to her, she was totally sunk.

"We're good, aren't we, Billy Jo?" Grant said with a hint of panic.

She didn't look away from Mark as she said, "Yeah, sure."

"Okay, good," Grant said. "Well, I'm going to pack up and head for the ferry. Billy Jo, send me the reports on the Gillespies." Then he walked away, faster than usual, and she spotted Pam following him, shooting her only a passing glance.

"Well, I didn't expect that," Billy Jo said. "You know I can fight my own battles, right?"

Mark didn't say anything at first, just reached for her and ran his hands over her shoulders. "I know you can. But he was grinding you into the ground, and I won't stand for that. He understands now."

She nodded. She'd never expected this kind of possessive alpha behavior for her. "Okay," she said, and his gaze flickered—from amusement, she thought.

"I got a call from the realtor," he said. "She has a house to show us."

"So you came because of the house?"

He glanced down the hall and then back to her, pulling her closer, settling her in his arms. "I came to make sure Grant understands my no-go zone, and now he does. The house is second. So what do you say we take a break and look at it?"

She pressed her hands to his chest, feeling more comfortable than she had in a long time. "Why not?" she said. "So does it have my kitchen, a yard for Lucky, and windows for Harley?"

He leaned in and kissed her, then pulled away and reached for her hand. "If it doesn't, we'll keep looking until we find one that does."

"That sounds good to me. So how many houses are we looking at?"

Mark linked his fingers with hers and pulled her with him to the door. "As many as it takes until we find the right one."

She made herself pull in a breath. "I think I already have," she said.

There was that smile as he leaned down and kissed her again, and when he pulled back, he pushed open the door and said, "So have I."

Chapter 16

"This is the third house we've looked at," Mark said, "so what exactly is it about this one that you don't like?"

Billy Jo made herself look around the open kitchen, with its small butcher block island, electric stove, and windows that didn't open. She didn't know why, but it just didn't feel right. "Other than the fact that it's overpriced? All the cars parked next door make it look like a junkyard, and I just don't want to live next to that. There's no wall oven, no gas stove…" She let out a sigh and looked around, not having to look over to know Mark was doing his best to stay calm.

"I ran a check on the neighbors," he said, "and we could do renovations."

Her cell phone was ringing, so she reached into her purse and pulled it out to see the caller was from the office. "Hi, Pam," she said, because it couldn't have been anyone else.

"We've got a problem," Pam said. "The military are here. They just walked in and are boxing up files. There are like twelve people, and they're going through everything, all the files. Do you know what the hell is going on? They're in your office."

Billy Jo turned to Mark, whose arms were crossed, looking rather annoyed, impatient. She let the phone slide away from her mouth. "Pam said the military are there, just walked in."

He frowned and uncrossed his arms, walking her way.

"Wait," Pam said. "One of them wants to know about a file for Deena Rae. It's not here."

She wasn't sure she could breathe. Mark was right in front of her, and she could hear voices in the background of the call. In that second, she was very aware that Deena Rae's file was inside the bulky purse over her shoulder.

"Why do they want her file?" she said. She had to turn away, as Mark was right in her face, waiting for her to say something.

"I don't know. I called Grant, but there was no answer. They want to talk to you."

"What? Pam, wait…"

"Ms. McCabe, this is Captain Dorsey. Ma'am, we're going to need you to return to the office right now."

Her heart thudded, because his voice made it clear it was an order. "Sure, on my way," she said, then hung up. "I've been ordered back to work. Pam said they're taking files, and they asked for Deena Rae's. I have it with me. I just can't give up trying to find her. It started with her. I know there has to be a link here, and—"

"Let's go," Mark said, not letting her finish. He touched her arm, and she started out past him. The realtor was by his Subaru, leaning against it, slender, balding, talking on his cell phone. "I'll call you," was all Mark said to him as they hurried to his Jeep.

Billy Jo climbed in and had just pulled her seatbelt on when Mark climbed behind the wheel and had the engine started.

"You said they want the file you have," he said. "While we're driving, get your phone out and take photos of everything in that file."

She didn't know why she hadn't thought of that. She reached for the file and her phone and opened it. "Mark, why would the military be here? They just showed up on the island for the files? I'm not an idiot. This is crazy."

He changed gears on the Jeep, driving fast toward town, which she could see in the distance. "I'd say it's because those kids disappeared under Mr. Stone's watch. Someone is cleaning up."

She paused. This wasn't what she'd wanted to hear. She was flipping pages and taking photos as he pulled around the corner into town and hit the brakes.

"Shit," he said, and when she looked up, her stomach pitched. Two Humvees were being filled, along with three black SUVs, and a lot of military personnel stood in front of the CPS office. Mark gestured to her. "Hurry up."

He put the Jeep back in gear and pulled into the lot as she took a photo of the last two pages, then closed up the file and tucked her phone back into her purse. Mark weaved around an SUV and parked off to the side in front of the industrial garbage bins. He tossed her a glance, and she was glad now that they'd left Lucky at the station, as her uneasiness made her worry what the hell they were walking into.

Mark turned off the Jeep, reached over to her, and touched her arm. "You don't offer anything. You give the file over but nothing else. Better yet, I'll talk. Say nothing."

Then he pulled open his door, and she followed, stepping out, taking her time as she walked around to where Mark was standing, his hands shoved in his pockets, waiting for her. His back was to her, but he held out a hand as she approached, glancing once to her with a grim expression.

"Give me the file," he said.

She hesitated only a second, the file in her hand, before she held it up and out to him, and he took it from her.

"Let's go." He started walking, and she fell in behind. A box was being carried out to one of the Humvees, the office door propped open. Mark tossed her an uneasy glance as he stepped inside, and there was Pam, wide eyed, with a lot of military guys.

"It's about time you got here," Pam said. "They just showed up, and they're taking apart the office.

They have a list of names and are taking those files. They just took right over…"

"Excuse me, are you Billy Jo McCabe? I'm Captain Dorsey," said a tall, solid man in military fatigues and a beret as he strode right to her. His eyes were hazel, she thought, and he had a strong jaw. He could go toe to toe with Mark. She didn't move.

"Yes, that's right. So what is this? Why are you taking files? You realize this isn't a military operation; this is CPS, Child Protective Services, where we look after children, at-risk kids. Yet you're walking out with our files?"

Damn, she was proud of herself for not backing down. At first, Dorsey didn't pull his gaze from her. Then he looked over to Mark, not fazed in the least. Evidently, strongminded women were nothing to him.

"This is now a military operation," he said, "and we've noted a missing file for Deena Rae."

Mark held it up, and Dorsey reached for it, then gave a sharp nod and walked back, holding his arm straight out to a military woman, her hair in a tight bun, packing up files.

She took it, stuck it in a box, and put a lid on it. "That was the last one, sir." She lifted the box. "Excuse me, ma'am," was all she said as she walked past Billy Jo out the door.

"Okay, we're done. Time to go," Captain Dorsey called out. Then someone walked past with her laptop.

"Hey, that's mine! You can't take it," Billy Jo yelled. She went to reach for it, but Dorsey and another military officer she hadn't seen stepped over to block her, reaching for her arm.

That was when everything went sideways.

"Get your hands off me!" She jerked her arm, which had been grabbed from behind.

"Let her go right now!" she heard Mark yell before she was slammed against the wall, her hand pulled behind her back. She heard the flick of the safety on a gun and turned her head, feeling the pain in her shoulder.

Mark was holding his gun straight at the captain, and another man in dark pants and a jacket was holding a gun at Mark. Her heart thudded as she stared in horror.

"Put the gun down now, Chief," the captain said, but Mark didn't look away, and she'd never seen him so determined. She couldn't move.

"Let go of me, please," she said even though she was scared shitless. The energy in the room had gone through the roof. "Mark, put it down. Stop, everyone, this is crazy. Take the damn computer."

"Your move, Chief," said Dorsey.

Billy Jo was still pressed to the wall, her arm pinned up. From the pain, she knew just one more inch and it would be dislocated.

"You first," Mark said, not looking her way. God damn, she'd never seen this side of him.

"Mark, please put the gun down," she said. "Let me go."

A second passed before Mark flicked the safety again, a hard expression on his face as he lifted the gun and held it out, other hand up. The officer took it, and the man who had held her against the wall let her go, another military guy with a dark face, dark hands, and dark eyes.

The captain only nodded, and the man who had Mark's gun emptied the rounds onto the carpet, emptied the chamber, and disassembled the gun before tossing it behind him in the garbage can.

What had passed between them was eerie, and her legs were shaking as they walked out, every one of them. Mark pulled her close, and she stumbled a bit.

"You okay?" He held her so tight she couldn't breathe.

"I'm fine, I'm fine… Mark, ease up. I can't breathe," she said, then pushed back, but he didn't let her go, running his hands over her. Pam was staring in horror.

Mark walked over to the door and pulled it closed, flicking the lock as the Humvees and SUVs pulled out. He touched her again, and she slapped her hand over his wrist, holding him.

"Well, that was a shitshow," she said.

He slid his arm over her shoulder again and pulled her close beside him. "You sure you're okay?"

She could only nod, furious. She was shaking so hard, which was something she never did.

Mark must have known, as he rubbed her arm. "He didn't hurt you?" He was looking down at her, and she made herself look up.

"I'll be okay. But we have more important things

to worry about, like that they took my computer but not my phone."

Mark pressed a kiss to her head, then walked over and squatted down to pick up his bullets and gun. Whoever that man was had disassembled it so quickly, but Mark took his time, looking at it and putting it back together.

"All right, first things first," Mark said. "Pam, can you make a list of every file they took?"

She'd never seen this expression on Pam's face before, but it was exactly how she felt.

"Pam, come on," Mark said again.

Pam gave her head a shake. "Sure."

Billy Jo walked over to where was Mark sliding the bullets back into his gun, and she set her hand over his arm. Pam was hurrying back to her desk. "He would have shot you, Mark."

He holstered his gun and pulled his hand over his face. "You think I'm going to let anyone put his hands on you?"

She couldn't say anything. She forced herself to nod. "So now what? What do you think that was about? You think every one of those files was one of Link Stone's, the missing kids?"

He let out a heavy sigh, thinking. "Yup, I think you're right," he said, then pulled out his phone.

"Who are you calling?"

He pressed the phone to his ear and looked down at her. "The military walks in here, onto my island, and I know nothing about it? I'm calling in help is what I'm doing."

She heard it ringing, and she glanced over to Pam at her desk before she thought she heard someone answer on the other end.

"Hey, it's Mark. You got a minute? Because I could use your help," he said, then only nodded. She didn't know who he was talking to. "Great. I'm at CPS. See you soon." Then he hung up.

She gestured wide. "Well?"

He pocketed his phone and glanced only once to Pam, who was still rattled. "I called Chief Shephard, because whatever our issues are, something sinister is going on. If I didn't know before, I do now. Nothing has ever happened on this island without Tolly Shephard knowing about it, and right now someone is playing a game, a dark and dangerous game. I have a feeling whatever Link Stone was involved in is linked to some pretty powerful people. In the meantime, can you give Pam a hand?"

She blew out a breath, needing to pull it together, and nodded. "Fine, but what are you going to do?"

He pulled his gun out and checked the rounds again, not something she'd seen him do before, then holstered it again. "I'm going to keep an eye out until Tolly gets here. Then I want whatever this is off my island."

Chapter 17

"It's every one of Link's files, even the ones where we know nothing happened to the kids," Billy Jo said. "Something is wrong here."

Pam was at her desk, Billy Jo was right there with her, and she was shaking her head. "It's not here," she said.

Billy Jo flicked her finger at the screen. "All of them?"

Pam typed something. "Every one of his files has been scrubbed from the system. Like, how is this possible? They're just gone…"

He heard the rattle of the front door, then the pounding, and Billy Jo's gaze flicked up with alarm. Damn, he was still trying to come down from his blinding rage because someone had lain a hand on his girl. He never pulled his gun if he didn't intend to use it, and his adrenaline was running.

He started to the door and took in the chief, Gail with him. He flicked the lock and then pushed the door open. "Thanks for coming down."

"Talk is all over town that the military showed up. The conspiracy theorists are talking about everything from military exercises on the island to a possible terrorist attack," Gail said, pressing her hand to his shoulder.

Mark gestured with his thumb to Billy Jo and Pam. "Not even close—but I have to say it's likely worse."

The chief locked the door, saying nothing.

"You have any idea why the military would show up here and take all Link Stone's files?" Mark asked him. "Now Pam is saying they've been wiped from the system. Maybe I should have asked you about Link Stone. You know anything about him and his time here, the money he took from kids, the checks? He's basically been tied to some pedo ring, trafficking and selling kids… Billy Jo, how many of the kids Link Stone placed disappeared?" He turned, fisting his hands once, twice. Damn, he couldn't remember the last time someone had ever put him this far over the edge. Fight or flight. He wouldn't back down.

"I found eight kids so far, but I think there were hundreds," Billy Jo called out. "No one followed up. You have any idea how many kids are here? Too many. Short of going around to visit all the time, how would anyone know they were even gone?"

"Oh, geez," Gail said, then shoved her hands in

her pockets and started across the room to Billy Jo and Pam. Mark dragged his gaze to the chief, who was staring at him long and hard.

"Yeah, I knew Link," he said, then gestured to Mark and took a few steps off to the side. He turned his back on the women, thought they were too far away to hear anyway. "He's off this island because I made him leave."

Mark really looked at the chief. "You knew he was selling kids?"

Tolly shook his head. "I told you before, Mark, that the things that happen on this island don't just happen here. This island is one of many places in this country where the elite have been doing things and getting away with them. I'm just one of many small-town sheriffs who know these people are virtually untouchable. When they do something, there isn't a trail you can follow to arrest them. But us small-town sheriffs are what stands between communities and those people, because they can do only so much until we find out."

Mark moved from side to side. "And you didn't call the Feds?"

Tolly Shephard looked at him as if he had said something really dumb. "I can see how unsettled you are. Can't blame you, but you need to pull it together, because the military don't show up and take things just because, not ever. And the Feds, are you kidding?" He made a rude sound and shook his head. "You're a smart man, Mark Friessen. I shouldn't have to explain to you how corrupt the DOJ is, and the FBI. No, you can't call them anymore, because they're deep into this, watching the backs of the elites. I shouldn't have to tell you who these people are—former and current heads of state and their families, bankers, judges, lawyers, Hollywood royals, real royals. They do despicable things, yet you can't touch them. You can't call anyone. But you can make sure you keep watch over your community. You think you can call the Feds and they're going to open an investigation?"

The chief sounded so pissed, and Mark didn't know what to say for a second. "You're telling me every federal agent is corrupt? Because I don't believe that."

He shook his head. "That's not what I'm saying, Mark. You may find that one agent, and they do exist, who'll start a file and investigate—until a big name is dropped and it crosses the boss's desk. Then the boss makes a call, a lot of suits walk in, the file is packed up, the case is closed, and that starry-eyed agent is reassigned to a field office in Duluth, and that's if he heeds the warning that there's nothing for him to investigate."

Mark looked past the old chief, over to Billy Jo. Maybe he just needed to make sure she was going to be okay. Maybe the chief had an idea of how scared he was.

"Word of advice, Mark, and I learned this the hard way. Save yourself. No matter what you think of me, the people of this island matter, and sometimes, to keep your community safe, you have to keep your job. If you rattle the wrong cage, those folks could appoint someone detrimental. I don't think I have to spell out to you what I'm talking about. You think I'm the only small-town cop who knows about this? Mark, come on. Many sheriffs are good people, good men, and will not look elsewhere when a bad element tries to slink into town. That's why, when I figured out what Link had done, I ran him off the island and shut down his sideline here."

He didn't know what to say. His heart was thudding. "And what about the kids? You didn't look for them?"

He knew he was being loud. Gail looked up and over to him, but the chief only pulled his arms across his chest and let out a heavy sigh. "It was March 11, three days before I cuffed Link to a chair and put a gun to his head. The kids were gone, all except one. I made a call to a friend I knew who worked for the Feds, then left Link in my basement for a day. When I got a call back, my friend said to let him go, because he'd received a call from the justice department, and a call like that means your family could suddenly disappear. I knew then how big this was. The only child I got back was a six-year-old little girl by the name of Teena. She was pretty messed up. I stood at the ferry the day he drove off the island."

Mark tried to understand what he was saying. "You know Link hanged himself, and San Antonio found a lot of kids, a lot of records. They're taking this ring down."

The chief let out a laugh he'd never heard before,

then shook his head. "Are you listening, Mark? The only ones they're getting are the middle men, the little guys, the ones who have become a liability. This is bigger, and until someone can cut off the head of the snake, that ring is untouchable."

$$\overline{\hspace{6cm}}$$

Chapter 18

$$\overline{\hspace{6cm}}$$

Billy Jo reached back to massage her shoulder, wincing from the sharp bite that had come out of nowhere. Strong hands touched her shoulders.

"Where does it hurt?" Mark said. His voice had an edge as he massaged the spot, and Billy Jo groaned, leaning her head back.

"Right there. Don't stop," she said as he leaned in and pressed a kiss to the back of her head. "So what were you and Tolly talking about over there? Seemed pretty intense."

"Trying to get ahead of whatever this is," Mark said as he kept massaging, and she just let her arms hang beside her as she stood near Pam's empty desk.

"And did you?"

He ran his hands over her shoulders and then stepped away, massage apparently done. "I take it every one of Link's cases has been scrubbed from the system?"

She'd never seen anything like this in her life. "As if they didn't even exist. Mark, this isn't right. I can't explain this, and I wouldn't believe any of it if I hadn't seen it with my own eyes. The only reason I know is because I was in the system on at least a dozen of those files the other day, searching, and they were there then. And what's really screwy is that Link Stone himself has been wiped from the system, as if he was never a social worker here."

She turned around and leaned against the desk. Pam was talking with Gail at the front door before she left. Of course she was upset, and so was Billy Jo.

"Someone's cleaning up," Mark said.

She flicked her gaze back over to him. "So how deep does this go? My dad showing up the way he did, you think I don't know what that was about? He couldn't pick up a phone? No. You know how I am about no one getting in my business, but he didn't want to talk on a phone, so he showed up here. Those kids who disappeared, it's pretty bad. What happened to them is worse than I can imagine. Are you keeping anything from me, Mark?"

There it was in his face. He couldn't hide anything. "How much do you want to know?"

She had to remind herself she could handle anything, and she could. She let her gaze fall away to the gun under his jean jacket, and she had to press her hands to her face. She'd never seen Mark go all cowboy the way he had. From the look on his face, she knew he'd have pulled the trigger.

"He would have shot you, Mark, and you'd have

taken the bullet. Link Stone wasn't the mastermind. Last year, more than four hundred thousand kids were taken by CPS just in this country. That's quite a pool of kids to have access to, and those kids don't really have anyone looking for them. These aren't kids from families with resources. So how deep do you think it goes? I'm well aware of how many sickos are out there. And one thing about them is that they love power. They aren't the creepy guy at the end of the street, like people think. They're polished, sophisticated, and can afford whatever sick, twisted things they want. And it isn't just men but women too, though most people would never believe it."

He appeared uncomfortable and pulled his arms over his chest, then ran a hand over the back of his head. "It's above my pay grade. I'm in unchartered territory here, Billy Jo. So when did you figure it out?"

What was she supposed to say? It had started when she was a kid, when she had figured out how disposable she was. She took in Gail and Tolly walking toward them.

"Okay, Pam is gone," Gail said. "Mark, I told Tolly he needs to share with you a group he's part of. They meet online."

Tolly gestured to Pam's desk and let out a heavy sigh as he walked around it and sat down, then looked over to Billy Jo. "You're going to have to log me in," he said, sliding the keyboard over to her.

"Okay, and should I ask why?" she replied as she typed in the password.

Tolly let his gaze linger on her. She knew he'd

never liked her, but there was something else there now. He was now typing, and she had to look away and over to Mark, who frowned and walked around her.

"Tolly is part of a group of small-town sheriffs across the country," Gail said.

Mark had his hand on her shoulder. Billy Jo wondered why this was the first time she was hearing of this.

"Hey there, Sal," Tolly said. "Here with me is Mark Friessen, who took over as the chief here on the island. I figured it's time you connected. The girl is Billy Jo McCabe, the new social worker. You probably already heard about the military showing up here, taking all the files, erasing every name from the system."

Billy Jo stared at the faces on the screen, a chat room. She made herself look back over to Tolly. Gail was still standing on the other side of the desk, her arms crossed. So much went on under the surface of this island that she was starting to think she and Mark had just been guests until now.

"No, I didn't hear, but check with TJ. I don't think he's here tonight. He said down in Texas there were some rumblings about an investigation into some missing girls, but, as usual, the Feds shut it down. Said it was scrubbed from the system, a lot of money. But this time he doesn't think it's going to get swept away."

Billy Jo narrowed her eyes and stared at the screen. She didn't know who was talking. She walked around the desk over to Gail, while Mark stood behind the chief with a lost look. Gail touched her arm and nodded across the room, and Billy Jo followed her there.

"Gail, what is this? A group of small-town sheriffs… Why? How?" She stopped, listening to the sheriffs talking. Mark was saying something, but she didn't know what.

"Tolly figured out a long time ago how corrupt the system is—the **DOJ**, the Feds. He says something changed noticeably ten years back, as if they'd become bolder. His words. The sheriffs, the local ones in small communities, they see a lot of stuff, but they get shut down when it's too big. The country has changed, and we're going the wrong way. He said there are more than three hundred sheriffs now in the group, and once they all started talking, sharing, they figured out they were running into the same thing. They talk to each other first now when something is happening under their noses in their counties. A lot of times, a federal judge will come in and overrule what a sheriff has done. They're finding out the problems they're having aren't isolated. It was one of the reasons Tolly walked Link Stone off this island."

She just stared at Gail, who gestured over to Mark, who was now sitting behind the desk. Tolly was walking their way. "Walked off the island? Why? How?"

"You ready?" Tolly said to Gail. "We got that dinner tonight." Then he looked down at Billy Jo and said, "Mark's now in the group, so he'll have an idea and a heads-up if any problems are coming his way. You tell her about Teena?"

Gail had an odd expression. "No. I was just telling Billy Jo how you walked Link Stone off the island. You told Mark?"

Tolly nodded. "He knows. Teena Baker, not sure if you'll still have a file on her considering Link was the social worker on record. She was the last one Link Stone took, and the only one who was found. She's back with her mother. She just started grade two. Gail, you want to fill her in? I'll go warm the truck," he said. Then he walked past her to the door, flicked open the lock, and walked out.

Billy Jo couldn't wrap her head around the bomb that had been dropped. "Uh, Gail, what?"

Gail looked back to her and then over to Mark, who was still talking, gesturing. "Tolly never expected policing would become political. I remember the day he figured out that putting someone away for a crime wasn't how it worked, not really. We get a lot of different people here on this island, more and more of whom are wealthy, with big estates, money. It takes things to a bigger scale. Tolly was the one who found Teena. She was on one of those supersized yachts, with a full crew. He arrested all of them, and an hour later it was pulling out of the harbour with the crew onboard. His hand was slapped, and he was told the Feds were handling it. You know how he found out?"

She stared at Gail, shaking her head.

"A tip. Someone on the inside, was all he could figure, who suddenly grew a conscience. You have

Mark call Tolly anytime he runs into something. Keep an eye on the kids, Billy Jo. Check them, double-check them, and don't let CPS come in and take them off the island. If they do, you make noise, a lot of noise. As you get to know the residents, you're going to figure out that there are two kinds here, those who give a damn and those who believe they can do anything to anyone at any time and no one can stop them. When you figure out who they are, you keep an eye on them." Then Gail lifted her hand. "Mark, we're leaving," she called out, then rubbed Billy Jo's shoulder and said, "Come over for dinner next week."

She walked to the door and pushed it open, and Billy Jo saw her out, still hearing Mark talking. She flicked the lock and watched as the chief pulled away, and she realized they'd only tapped the surface of what the chief and Gail knew about what was really going on on the island.

Chapter 19

Mark wanted this to be perfect. He waited for Billy Jo, who was in the master bedroom of the house Gail had sent him a link to, and stared at the text from her dad, a man who had shown up and left as quickly as he'd arrived.

Well, does she like it?

Later. We'll talk later, he texted back, then pocketed his phone.

He took in the white cabinets, the big windows, an open kitchen with everything he knew she wanted. The house had three bedrooms, a den, a yard, and no neighbors they could see.

Billy Jo walked out of the bedroom, her arms crossed, wearing a familiar frown—but damn, he wanted some happiness out of this shitstorm he could feel swirling around him.

"You haven't said anything," he told her. "You know that's the perfect padded window seat for

Harley. He can sleep and stare out the window all day. And the yard, well, it's an acre, so there's plenty of room for Lucky. There's even a garden. It's quiet, a dead-end street. The shower in the master could fit three, easily, and the kitchen…" He gestured.

She was still not smiling, and he could see the edge, the tension. But he knew it was because they'd had their eyes opened to too much, and it had been unexpected.

"How much, again?" she said. "Gail sent this?"

He wondered how many excuses she'd come up with as to why this couldn't work. "In our budget. And yes, it's someone Gail knows. Come on, what's there not to love about this place?"

She made a face and shrugged.

He reached into his pocket, gripping the small box, reminding himself he was in uncharted territory. When he walked over to her, went down on one knee, and flicked the box open, her face, her eyes, her expression were priceless.

"Okay, I'm going out on a limb here," he said, "but I'm done dancing around after everything we've been through. I want to keep doing it together with you, so, Billy Jo McCabe, will you marry me?"

She lifted her hands to her cheeks and flicked those blue eyes to him. Damn, she was gorgeous—and rattled. "That's a ring," she said.

"It is, and it set me back some. Could you answer me so I can get up?" The floor was hard, and his knee was starting to ache.

She reached out and touched the ring, then looked at him again. "You want to marry me?"

He sensed the second this could go sideways. "Very much."

"Like, forever?"

He pressed his other hand to the floor and stood up, then took the ring from the box, which he tossed to the floor. He reached for her hand and slipped it on the tip of her finger. "Like, forever. You and me, Lucky, Harley, and this house…"

She slid her hand over his and the ring on her finger, and she nodded. "Yes, Mark, I would very much like to marry you."

He lifted her and swung her around, and her laughter was something he didn't hear often. He put her down and kissed her once, then again, and reached for her hand, seeing the three small diamonds. He looked across the kitchen. "And the house?"

She squeezed his hand and nodded. "Yes to the house, too. I think it will work."

"Well, that's good, because I already put down a deposit."

She lifted a brow, and he pulled her close again, his arms around her. He wondered if this was what his brothers had felt before they'd started a new chapter with their wives.

"So when can we move in?" she said.

He went to lean in and kiss her again, but she pressed her hands to his chest. "A few weeks, give or take," he replied. "What about the wedding?" He expected her to stiffen, to step back, to walk away.

"After we move in here, after I talk to my parents," she said. "You think we can do this?"

He hesitated only a second. "I know we can."

Turn the page for a sneak peek of
*THE LAST STAND the next book in the BILLY JO
MCCABE MYSTERY*
Available in print, eBook & audio

Coming next in the Billy Jo
McCabe Mystery

The law is the law until someone comes after your family.

From *New York Times* & *USA Today* bestselling author Lorhainne Eckhart comes a new Billy Jo McCabe mystery set on a small island town in the Pacific Northwest. On the eve of Police Chief Mark Friessen's wedding, a fierce snowstorm blankets the island, knocking out power, and the body of a woman is discovered in the church. The only clue is the note in her hand, a list of names—all members of Mark's family.

Mark Friessen has been counting down the days to his wedding to Billy Jo McCabe. Yet only days from Christmas, after their families arrive, a freak blizzard comes out of nowhere and knocks out power on the entire island.

With the island in an emergency and the ferry shut down, no help is arriving anytime soon from the mainland. Mark receives a call to stop into the church where he and Billy Jo are planning on being married the next day, but there he stumbles upon the body of a woman. The only evidence is a note she's clutching. At the top, in all bold, is the word *KILL*, and listed below are the names of everyone he loves, including Billy Jo, his parents, his brothers, their wives, and his two nieces.

With access to the outside world cut off, Mark finds himself up against an invisible enemy who he believes is coming after his unsuspecting family. But Mark has no idea who it is. Where is the killer hiding on the island, why isn't Mark's name on the list, and who is the dead woman? Mark is determined to find the killer and protect his family, whatever it takes…even if it's his *Last Stand*.

Mark stared at the weekly report of problems, a revolving door of the same people, those he could do something about and those who just got better at hiding their crimes. He heard the knock on his door just as he took a swallow of coffee, and he turned where he was standing beside his desk.

"Hey, Chief," said Carmen. "Just got a call from Lisa Jenkins about a man who's openly threatening her. His hostility is over the top, so much so that she fears for her safety. She said she showed up for a wellness check on his kids and believes he's hurting them and interfering with her taking them."

He just stared at Carmen as she shrugged on her heavy coat, wondering whether he was supposed to know who Lisa Jenkins was. Maybe his expression gave him away. He set down the printed three-page report, which had been waiting on his desk when he walked in an hour earlier.

"Taking kids, wellness checks? You lost me. Who is

this?" He let out a heavy sigh, feeling the weight of everything. His parents were on their way, his brothers, their families, and Billy-Jo's family. He still needed to pay the restaurant, pick up his new suit, and make sure he stopped in at the church at some point that day to make sure everything was a go for the wedding. He gave his head a shake, willing himself to get back in the game.

"Lisa…" Carmen said. "You know, the junior social worker brought in to help with the rise in the case load? For your fiancée."

Right. He thought Billy Jo had mentioned that at the church before their meeting with the minister who would listen as they said "I do" and officially pronounce them mister and missus. Maybe that was why he was feeling a gigantic pressure right in the middle of his chest. Mark reached for his cell phone on his desk but saw no message from Billy Jo.

"Billy Jo didn't call," he said. "Is she there too?" He had his phone to his ear already, and it was ringing, but it went right to voicemail.

"Hello, this is Billy Jo McCabe, with DCFS. I can't take your call right now. Leave me a message and I'll call you back when I can. If this is an emergency…"

He hung up. Right, she wasn't going in to work that day because Chase and Rose were flying in, and she was doing all the last-minute stuff involving her dress and something else he couldn't remember.

He realized Carmen was still standing there. "No answer." He held his phone up. "I'll come with you.

Have you met this Lisa?" He reached for his keys in his drawer and shoved his phone in his pocket, looking to Carmen as he strode over to the coat tree and reached for his black down winter coat. His gun was holstered on his favorite blue jeans, and his sheriff's badge was pinned to his shirt.

"Only once," she said. "She's young. Don't think she's been doing this long. You want to follow me?"

Mark shrugged on his coat. "Yeah. So tell me again who she is and what's going on. Would have thought this would go through Billy Jo. You said this social worker is taking the kids? She's supposed to call us first, or have I missed something?"

Carmen had already pulled open the door to the station and was walking out. A blast of cold swept over him as he glanced back to his dog's empty bed. Billy Jo had Lucky at home. Maybe that was also why he felt so off that day. His routine was being completely screwed up.

"Lacy," he called out.

"I already know," the dispatcher replied. "I took the call and patched it through to Carmen." She was behind her desk, Gail's old desk, and she gestured to him as she stood up. So damn efficient, but he wondered when he'd stop comparing her to Gail. "You'll be at the Clarks'. I got it." She just lifted her hand, and Mark took in Elisha's empty desk, as well, knowing she was already doing rounds on the island.

"Well, good," he said. "If Billy Jo calls, tell her to call me."

He didn't miss what he thought was the hint of a

smile tugging at the older woman's lips. Her hair was a mix of dark and white, and he was pretty sure she was as tall as Gail.

He stepped out of the office and kept walking down the steps, feeling the icy chill. The salt on the steps crunched under his cowboy boots. Heavy clouds loomed overhead, but he knew it was too cold for rain.

Carmen was already in the sheriff's cruiser as Mark pulled open the door of his Jeep and started the engine. Carmen backed out, swinging around and flicking on her siren. So they were there, kids in trouble, a desperate situation. Damn, he hated that. He wished Billy Jo had filled him in more on this Lisa.

He followed Carmen as she pulled down a road he was familiar with and took in the houses so close together. Cars pulled over to the side as they flew past another road, more trees and privacy. Carmen pulled up in front of a small older two-story. He could see a man in the doorway, dark skinned, tall, lanky, and a woman on the porch.

Carmen was parked behind a burgundy Hyundai, and Mark stopped in front, turning off his engine, feeling his sidearm. He stepped out of the Jeep, his coat now zipped, and reached for his brown knit hat in his pocket. As he pulled it on, feeling the bite of cold, he strode across the grass, Carmen already two steps ahead of him.

"Thank goodness you're here," the young woman said. "This man is preventing me from doing my job.

He's openly harassed me and been verbally abusive…"

"I did no such thing, you lying bitch. You showed up here, coming in my house, disrespecting me," the man cut in. He wore a long-sleeved faded brown shirt and what looked like sweatpants. He had no coat. Mark figured the woman was Lisa, who had called.

"Okay, so what exactly is going on here?" Mark said, resting his foot on the bottom step.

Lisa was young, early twenties, he thought, wearing dark-rimmed glasses and holding a clipboard close to her chest. He glanced once to Carmen, who appeared right beside him. Mark was very aware of the man's anger toward Lisa. He stepped up onto the porch, looking down on her, putting himself between them.

"And you are?" he said to the man.

"That's Nathan Clark," Lisa cut in behind him, and he didn't miss the snark in her tone. He glanced back once to her, knowing Nathan was fisting his hands. Just her opening her mouth had provoked him.

He turned back to Nathan, who looked past him with dark eyes locked on to the short social worker. He knew when a man had been pushed too far. "Nathan, I'm Chief Friessen. We got a call about some trouble…"

The man was already shaking his head and had pulled his arms across his chest. He had to be cold. Mark took in the closed screen door and could hear voices inside, a woman and kids, he thought.

"Look, I don't know what she's yapping on about,

but she showed up here, walking through my house, and yelled at me to get away from her when I did nothing. She was the one disrespecting me and my wife. She's going on about us hurting our kids, which is an outright lie…"

"I'm just doing my job," Lisa said. "You have no right to interfere, and that was exactly what you were doing in there, following me right on my heels and yelling at me, scaring me. This is a state matter, and you are interfering—"

"These are my kids," Nathan said. "You coming in here, turning your nose up at me and—"

"Hey, hey, enough," Mark said. "Just cool down, both of you. Nathan, give us a minute." He turned to the new social worker and wondered why Billy Jo hadn't called him. "Come with me. I want to talk to you."

He went down the steps, seeing her legs were bare under her coat. She wore a short dress underneath, he thought, and light brown ankle boots. He gestured to her and then took in Carmen, who said nothing as she stood there. He had only to nod before he heard her say something to the father, who was standing guard at that door.

He turned around, taking in how short Lisa was, about Billy Jo's height. She really looked like a kid. "What's going on here? Billy Jo sent you?" They were far enough away that he couldn't hear what the father was saying to Carmen, but he could see how upset he was.

"I'm the social worker on call today, and this is a

wellness check. A complaint came in, and it was given to me. This has nothing to do with Billy Jo, who's away now. Everything will come through me until she's back from her time off."

The way she was looking at him, he realized she didn't have a clue who she was, but then, he knew Billy Jo didn't go around sharing her personal business. Evidently, Lisa wasn't in the know.

"Billy Jo is getting married to me. I'm her fiancé. You should know, filling in for her, that we have a protocol on the island. In any cases where you're removing a child, you are required to contact my office, and a deputy is to accompany you." He kept his voice low.

When she looked up at him, he could see she wasn't on the same page, maybe because she was shaking her head. "With all due respect, Chief, this was not a visit where I planned to take the kids. But, just showing up here and seeing what I saw, I'm alarmed. The condition of the premises, the dirt, the locked doors…and there was feces on the floor. The father is volatile, and the kids appear unbathed. One little girl, who I understand has special needs, appears neglected." She was so damn matter of fact, and he sensed she would argue about everything.

"Volatile? I think you need to be a little more specific about what your concerns are. You suspect abuse, hurting his kids?" He gestured, wondering why she had a clipboard.

"You saw him up there, the way he looked at me, yelling at me. He stalked behind me in the house when I expected answers from him. He was disrespectful…"

Mark angled his head. He wanted to call Billy Jo again, but if he did, he knew her well enough to know she'd likely be in her car and on her way over there. Maybe there was something more about this situation that he didn't know.

"You showed up here about his kids. I'm seeing a father who's trying to protect them. You want to take his kids away? I would be surprised if a father let you do that without fighting back. You want to walk me inside and show me what the issues are?"

The way she pulled the clipboard up close to her chest, he wondered if she'd say no. "Fine, but I'll need your assistance getting the kids out of the house. This is a state decision, and I'm acting on behalf of the state. I'll need to take the kids, all of them, to the hospital for a doctor to look them over."

Then she turned and started walking back to the house, and Mark followed, seeing that Carmen and Nathan were staring at him long and hard.

"I'm going in the house with Lisa," he said. "Nathan, Carmen will stay outside with you. We won't be a minute."

Lisa had pulled open the screen and walked right in, and Mark reached for the door.

Nathan lifted his hands in the air and linked them behind his head in frustration. "Fine. My wife is there."

"How many kids?" he asked. He could hear Lisa

inside, speaking with the kind of voice that expected answers, but about what, he didn't know.

"Two girls, two and five," Nathan said.

He only nodded and walked inside, taking in the small entry, the wood floors, an older sectional with piles of clothes on it, a laundry basket, toys and papers scattered on the floor. A woman with dark hair, a few inches taller than Lisa, was holding a towel. Her hair was half out of a ponytail.

"Down here, Chief," Lisa said to him as she gestured to a narrow hall with doors closed. He only nodded at the woman standing there, wide-eyed, a little girl jumping around her with a thumb in her mouth. Then he realized another girl was there, naked, her hair a mess, shoving ripped paper into her mouth.

"No, no, no, Mellie," the woman said and ran over to the little girl to pull the paper from her mouth. The girl squealed and swatted at her.

Mark saw the mother struggling, and he took in something smeared on the wall in the hall. He could smell it from there and knew it was feces. The social worker was looking at him expectantly as she stood by a door locked with a deadbolt, which needed a key, and another door with a sliding bolt.

"Every door here, all four, has a lock on it," Lisa said. "Do they lock the kids in? I'm sure you can smell that a child defecated, and it's on the walls. One has no clothes on, and there's something wrong with the other, too. The place is a mess. The kitchen is not the neatest I've seen, and there's food in the corner on the floor."

He slid the bolt on one of the doors and opened it to see a bathroom—not a mess but reasonable, with a towel on a hook, toothbrushes by the sink, and a bathtub with no shower curtain.

"Look, I don't know what to say," Mark said. "I see the mess. Is there something wrong with the one screaming out there?" He glanced down the hall. Everything in the house felt tense, but then, he supposed having DCFS show up like this only ramped up family problems.

"Special needs, I think. Not really sure, but something is wrong…" She was flipping through her chart, lifting papers and reading, and then she shook her head and let out an exasperated breath. "But, regardless, the care is seriously lacking. I'll need some help getting the kids loaded up. I think I've seen enough here." She clutched her clipboard to her chest. The way she said it had been dismissive, and damn, did he hate this. She brushed past him, leaving him standing there.

"Okay, I'm taking the kids," she said. "Are there car seats? I need clothes on these girls, too…"

She was cold, unfeeling. Nothing about this felt right. The mother wore a look he knew too well, shell-shock. He put his hand on the screen door and pushed it open, and Nathan and Carmen both stopped talking and looked at him.

"Your kids in there," he said. "Something wrong with the little girl with no clothes on?"

The man was much calmer now. He wondered what Carmen had said to him. "My older one, she's five. One doctor said she's got autism, another said rett syndrome. Can't keep no clothes on her. She takes them off as soon as they're on."

Mark realized Carmen hadn't looked away from Nathan, yet she said nothing. "You have locks on the doors in there. You lock the kids in?"

Nathan shook his head and gestured. "No, sir, no way. Those locks are to keep Mellie out. She wears a diaper, but we can't keep it on her. We lock the doors because she goes in and wipes her shit on the walls everywhere, so we have to keep her in one small part of the house. Look, we're doing the best we can, but I'm not always here. I have to work off island a lot, and it's just my wife here. My daughter, she screams if you try to brush her hair. Can't get socks on her at all. I tried to explain all that to the social worker in there, but she wouldn't hear none of it…"

"Hey, Nathan, I get it," Carmen cut in. "You just need some help, is all. Sometimes these state workers only check boxes and can't see or hear anything. I know you're just trying to protect your family, and I can hear how upset you are. She probably didn't understand all that. She's not from around here and doesn't know you."

Damn, how did Carmen do that? The door squeaked open behind them.

"Chief Friessen, I'm ready to go," Lisa said. "Can you get some car seats so I can take the kids?" There was something so inexperienced about the social worker. She had so much to learn about people.

"I have car seats, but I want the name of your supervisor," Nathan said.

Lisa was still standing in the doorway. "My direct supervisor is away right now. You want the name of my acting supervisor this week?" Now she sounded way too helpful.

"I do, name and phone number. I'm calling and making a formal complaint about you."

He wondered whether Lisa would say no, but she only shrugged and said, "Sure. Grant—"

"Billy Jo is in charge here. Pretty sure you report to her," Mark couldn't help himself from saying.

Lisa seemed to stiffen and then shook her head. "Ms. McCabe is away, and that's not how the chain of command works. Grant is who I report to right now." Damn, she was so matter of fact. "You have a pen?"

Carmen, bless her, pulled one from her pocket along with paper and handed it to Nathan, who was going to have his kids pulled out of there. Mark listened to her rattle off Grant's name and number.

"I'll help you with the car seats," Mark said to Nathan. He listened to screaming in the house as he followed him down the stairs and over to an older off-white minivan, and all he could think was that nothing about this seemed right.

About the Author

"Lorhainne Eckhart is one of my go to authors when I want a guaranteed good book. So many twists and turns, but also so much love and such a strong sense of family."

(Lora W., Reviewer)

New York Times & USA Today bestseller Lorhainne Eckhart writes Raw Relatable Real Romance is best known for her big family romances series, where "Morals and family are running themes. Danger, romance, and a drive to do what is right will see you glued to the page." As one fan calls her, she is the "Queen of the family saga." (aherman) writing "the ups and downs of what goes on within a family but also with some suspense, angst and of course a bit of romance thrown in for good measure." Follow Lorhainne on Bookbub to receive alerts on New Releases and Sales and join her mailing list at LorhainneEckhart.com for her Monday Blog, books news, giveaways and FREE reads. With over 120 books, audiobooks, and multiple series published and available at all retailers now translated into six languages. She is a multiple recipient of the Readers' Favorite Award for Suspense and Romance, and lives in the Pacific Northwest on an island, is the mother of three, her oldest has autism and she is an advocate for never giving up on your dreams.

"Lorhainne Eckhart has this uncanny way of just hitting the spot every time with her books."

(Caroline L., Reviewer)

The O'Connells: *The O'Connells of Livingston, Montana are not your typical family. A riveting collection of stories surrounding the ups and downs of what goes on within a family but also with some suspense, angst and of course a bit of romance thrown in for good measure "I thought I loved the Friessens, but I abso-*

lutely adore the O'Connell's. Each and every book has totally different genres of stories but the one thing in common is how she is able to wrap it around the family which is the heart of each story."
(C. Logue)

The Friessens: *An emotional big family romance series, the Friessen family siblings find their relationships tested, lay their hearts on the line, and discover lasting love! "Lorhainne Eckhart is one of my go to authors when I want a guaranteed good book. So many twists and turns, but also so much love and such a strong sense of family." (Lora W., Reviewer)*

The Parker Sisters: *The Parker Sisters are a close-knit family, and like any other family they have their ups and downs. "Eckhart has crafted another intense family drama…The character development is outstanding, and the emotional investment is high…" (Aherman, Reviewer)*

The McCabe Brothers: *Join the five McCabe siblings on their journeys to the dark and dangerous side of love! An intense, exhilarating collection of romantic thrillers you won't want to miss. —*

"Eckhart has a new series that is definitely worth the read. The queen of the family saga started this series with a spin-off of her wildly successful Friessen series." From a Readers' Favorite award—winning author and "queen of the family saga" (Aherman)

Lorhainne loves to hear from her readers! You can connect with me at:
www.LorhainneEckhart.com
lorhainneeckhart.le@gmail.com

Also by Lorhainne Eckhart

The Outsider Series
The Forgotten Child (Brad and Emily)
A Baby and a Wedding *(An Outsider Series Short)*
Fallen Hero (Andy, Jed, and Diana)
The Search *(An Outsider Series Short)*
The Awakening (Andy and Laura)
Secrets (Jed and Diana)
Runaway (Andy and Laura)
Overdue *(An Outsider Series Short)*
The Unexpected Storm (Neil and Candy)
The Wedding (Neil and Candy)

The Friessens: A New Beginning
The Deadline (Andy and Laura)
The Price to Love (Neil and Candy)
A Different Kind of Love (Brad and Emily)
A Vow of Love, A Friessen Family Christmas

The Friessens
The Reunion
The Bloodline (Andy & Laura)
The Promise (Diana & Jed)
The Business Plan (Neil & Candy)
The Decision (Brad & Emily)
First Love (Katy)
Family First

Leave the Light On
In the Moment
In the Family
In the Silence
In the Charm
Unexpected Consequences
It Was Always You
The First Time I Saw You
Welcome to My Arms
Welcome to Boston
I'll Always Love You
Ground Rules
A Reason to Breathe
You Are My Everything
Anything For You
The Homecoming
Stay Away From My Daughter
The Bad Boy
A Place of Our Own
The Visitor
All About Devon
Long Past Dawn
How to Heal a Heart
Keep Me In Your Heart

The O'Connells
The Neighbor
The Third Call
The Secret Husband
The Quiet Day
The Commitment

The Missing Father
The Hometown Hero
Justice
The Family Secret
The Fallen O'Connell
The Return of the O'Connells
And The She Was Gone
The Stalker
The O'Connell Family Christmas
The Girl Next Door
Broken Promises
The Gatekeeper

The McCabe Brothers
Don't Stop Me (Vic)
Don't Catch Me (Chase)
Don't Run From Me (Aaron)
Don't Hide From Me (Luc)
Don't Leave Me (Claudia)
Out of Time

A Billy Jo McCabe Mystery
Nothing As it Seems
Hiding in Plain Sight
The Cold Case
The Trap
Above the Law
The Stranger at the Door
The Children
The Last Stand

The Street Fighter
Finding Home

The Wilde Brothers
The One (Joe and Margaret)
The Honeymoon, A Wilde Brothers Short
Friendly Fire (Logan and Julia)
Not Quite Married, A Wilde Brothers Short
A Matter of Trust (Ben and Carrie)
The Reckoning, A Wilde Brothers Christmas
Traded (Jake)
Unforgiven (Samuel)
The Holiday Bride

Married in Montana
His Promise
Love's Promise
A Promise of Forever

The Parker Sisters
Thrill of the Chase
The Dating Game
Play Hard to Get
What We Can't Have
Go Your Own Way
A June Wedding

Kate & Walker
One Night
Edge of Night
Last Night

Walk the Right Road Series
The Choice
Lost and Found
Merkaba
Bounty
Blown Away: The Final Chapter

The Saved Series
Saved
Vanished
Captured

Single Titles
He Came Back
Loving Christine

For my German Readers
Die Außenseiter-Reihe
Der Vergessene Junge
Der Gefallene Held

For my French Readers
L'ENFANT OUBLIÉ

9 781990 590238